## "Richard, I'm sorry."

He turned and leaned against the countertop. "Grace, I am not hurt or offended. I hope I didn't offend you by extending such an offer."

She bowed her head and shook it. "No, I was not offended."

"But you're still hoping for romantic love."

She raised her gaze and caught his lively blue-green eyes and smiled. "Yes, I guess I am."

He crossed his arms. "Grace, I am not a romantic man. And while I would—" he cleared his throat "—want a real marriage, I've come to accept that is not a part of my future."

She reached over and touched his lips with her finger. They were warm, soft... She removed her finger. "Richard, I do not wish to hear you put yourself down in such a manner again. You are far more than you believe yourself to be."

She stepped away and walked toward the stove, across the room from where he stood. "I'll do it," she said, keeping her back to him. "I'll marry you."

**Books by Lynn A. Coleman**

Love Inspired Heartsong Presents

*Courting Holly*
*Winning the Captain's Heart*
*The Innkeeper's Wife*

## *LYNN A. COLEMAN*

is an award-winning and bestselling author and the founder of the American Christian Fiction Writers organization. She makes her home in Keystone Heights, Florida, where her husband of forty years serves as pastor of Friendship Bible Church. Together they are blessed with three children, two living and one in glory, and eight grandchildren.

LYNN A. COLEMAN

# The Innkeeper's Wife

HEARTSONG
PRESENTS

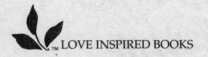 LOVE INSPIRED BOOKS

ISBN-13: 978-0-373-48732-5

The Innkeeper's Wife

Copyright © 2014 by Lynn A. Coleman

www.Harlequin.com

Printed in U.S.A.

Trust in the Lord with all thine heart;
and lean not unto thine own understanding.
—*Proverbs* 3:5

# *Chapter 1*

*St. Augustine, FL, 1871*

"**Y**ou're fired!" Richard Arman's voice echoed through the alley as Grace Martin pulled up to the side door of the Seaside Inn with her handcart filled with fresh linens. Mr. Arman was one of her newer clients and she'd never heard such anger and exasperation from him before. He tended to keep conversations at a minimum. She wondered what had him riled.

A thunder of pots and pans tossed out the window caused Grace to stop short and wait until the commotion ended. Soon Mr. Arman's cook, Jorge, came out into the street stomping and muttering under his breath. He made no note of Grace's presence and headed in the opposite direction, tearing off his apron as he strode away from the shore toward town.

Grace paused and said a prayer. She needed to deliver the clean linens, but she also wanted Mr. Arman to have a moment to compose himself.

Another voice, female, split the air. "You are a..." she shrieked in English, completing the sentence in Spanish with a string of expletives.

Having grown up in St. Augustine, Grace could hold her own with the Spanish tongue. Unfortunately, some of the earliest words she'd learned as a child were swearwords. And the language spewing from this woman at Mr. Arman was some of the vilest she'd heard in a long time.

"I quit!" Eva, Mr. Arman's chambermaid, exited the same side door as Jorge. Eva stood about Grace's own height of five feet five inches. The woman glared at Grace. "What are you looking at?"

Grace said nothing. Eva tended to be easily angered and sometimes even bullied the patrons. Eva cocked her head arrogantly and headed off in the same direction as Jorge.

Before Grace had time to think, the tall, thin frame of Richard Arman appeared in the back alley doorway. He stepped out and picked up the pots that had been tossed out. He glanced at Grace and mumbled, "Sorry."

Grace chose not to comment on what had transpired, smiled, lifted her handcart and took the last few steps to the door. "I have your order here. I'll set them in the linen closet, and you can pay me next week."

"Nonsense. You should not be burdened with a bad day just because I have had one. Give me a moment and I'll settle our account, Mrs. Martin."

"Thank you, Mr. Arman."

Grace picked up the first bundle of clean white sheets and walked through the kitchen to the back-room linen closet. The original house had been built around a hundred years before, with more recent additions dating from long before she'd been born. Placing the linens in the closet, she worked her way back to the kitchen and examined the mess the cook had left behind. A blob of some sort of stew dripped down the counter into a growing puddle on the floor.

Grace tried to ignore the mess and continue her work. She was the laundress and nothing more. She'd taken over the business from her good friend Mercy Hastings. Actually, she was Mercy Darling now, since she'd married a month ago and settled on Cape Cod, Massachusetts, with her new husband.

Grace thought back on the whirlwind romance that developed between Mercy and Wyatt. Their romance was nothing like hers and Micah's. Theirs had grown since she was thirteen and he was fourteen. She and Micah had loved each other all through their school days. And when he decided to go fight in sixty-four, they married and had only six weeks together before he left. She had written letters to him every day. Some he received, some he didn't. The worst letter she'd received had been the one announcing that Micah had died in battle. Grace's heart still ached just thinking about it.

She swept away the painful images and collected the rest of the linens. Now was not the time to get lost in the past. Once the linens were placed neatly in the cupboard, she closed the doors and entered the kitchen again. The mess on the floor needed to be cleaned up, and Richard Arman was nowhere in sight. Without much thought, she gathered some rags and a sponge to clean up the mess. After the majority of the spill was off the floor, she used a damp cloth to clean the rest. Working on her hands and knees, she wiped and rinsed the rag again and again.

"Mrs. Martin, that is not your position."

"I am well aware of that, Mr. Arman. But it seemed prudent to lend a hand. Which is precisely what I am doing."

"Forgive me," he sighed. "It has been one of those days."

*Apparently.* She held her tongue.

"Thank you for your kindness."

"You are welcome."

He held out his hand, offering a small yellow envelope. "This should satisfy my debt. Did you gather the soiled linens?"

"No, sir. I didn't see any in the basket."

Richard Arman inhaled deeply then let it out slowly. "If you have a moment, I shall gather them for you."

Grace nodded. Richard Arman was a handsome man with his brown hair, green-blue eyes and a not-too-square chin, yet not overly rounded or pointy, either. Today she saw a hardness in him she'd never seen before. No, that wasn't it exactly. It was more like a stiffness, an uncertainty in his actions. He was upset, and his posture showed it. She sent another prayer heavenward on behalf of Mr. Arman. She had no idea what had transpired between his employees and himself, but whatever it was, it had a tremendous impact. Obviously, losing both the cook and the chambermaid would have a profound effect on the inn.

She finished wiping up the floor and counter then rinsed the rags out for him. She could add those to her load, as well.

Richard Arman slipped through the open door with

a bundle of sheets and towels. "Forgive me for the delay to your schedule, Mrs. Martin."

"It is not a problem." She wouldn't be set back more than thirty minutes, leaving plenty of time to do the laundry before dinner. He handed her the bundle. "Shall I carry it outside for you?"

"Thank you, but I'll manage. God's blessings, Mr. Arman. I'll be praying for you."

"Thank you, I'll need your prayers," Richard grumbled. "Forgive me, I am in a rather sour disposition this morning." He turned and left the kitchen, presumably to go back to his office.

Grace realized he would need to perform the duties of the chambermaid and the cook. Although, if she remembered correctly, the inn only supplied a morning fare for the boarders. Grace shrugged and went on her way. She had plenty of work to do, and there was no sense in lollygagging.

Richard watched Grace Martin load her handcart and begin rolling it down the alley back to the street in front of the house. She was a fine-looking young woman, with blond hair and the most wonderful pair of chocolate-brown eyes he'd ever seen. As best as he'd been able to figure out, she was a widow and frustrated living with her parents. Her laundry business kept her busy and gainfully employed, but he wondered if she truly earned enough to be on her own with a yard and barn big enough to dry the sheets and towels for her clients.

She did fine work. He never had a complaint...unlike Eva and Jorge. Those two had needed to be fired. He had tried working with them, but today was the last straw. He suspected Jorge had been stealing from him, but to find him actually making a lamb stew in Richard's own kitchen and selling it behind his back, that was too much. Eva seemed to be a part of it, as well. He still wasn't certain how she was involved, but her quitting didn't make much difference. Now he needed to hire two more employees. He could handle the morning breakfast for a while. Cleaning chamber pots, on the other hand, making beds, cleaning the rooms…they were not his favorite part of the job. He could do the tasks…just not as efficiently as he would like.

The bell over the front door jangled. Richard glanced at the clock. It was nearly 11 a.m., and he was behind. He closed his eyes, fired off a prayer and thanked the Lord for Grace's prayers on his behalf. He entered the front parlor. A sailor with burly shoulders faced him, his feet spread apart, signifying that slight difference that spoke volumes about a person who spent more time on the sea than on dry land. "How may I help you?"

"Heard you rent rooms to sailors."

"Yes, sir. I have a room available. I charge a dollar a night and another if you would like breakfast in the morning."

"Just the night. I won't be needing breakfast."

"Very well. Would you sign here, please?" Richard pointed to the guest register on the counter. The register was an addition he added when he started working for his grandmother. It gave the inn a more professional air, as opposed to the feel of spare rooms rented from a private home. In fact, the Seaside Inn had a wing with six rooms on the top floor and six rooms on the bottom. At one time, a section of the house had been strictly reserved for his grandparents' family. Now Richard rented some of those rooms, as well.

The young sailor pulled off his cap, brushed his hair back and signed the book with his left hand. Richard glanced at the name. "Pleasure to have you with us, Mr. Davis."

"Pleasure's mine. If you don't mind, I'd like to dump my gear and see if I can pick up another job and sail out in the morning."

"I understand. Up the stairs, second door on your right."

"Thank you." He hefted his duffel bag up over his shoulder and took the stairs two at a time.

Richard scanned the layer of dust collecting on the tables. He had his work cut out for him. Why had he ever considered running this inn to begin with? He had come to help his grandmother when she was beginning to fail and his personal life was in shambles. And, truth be told, he enjoyed working the inn and meeting people. His grandparents ran the inn for forty years. The last year of her life, Grandma Arman was in declining health, and he had stepped in to handle the boarders. He glanced out the front bay window and scanned the harbor. He loved the view. It brought back many memories as a kid spending his summer vacations with his grandparents.

The thundering steps of Mr. Davis rattled down the stairway. "Excuse me, but word on the docks is that a sailor was beaten and had his entire life savings stolen a few months back. Did the sheriff catch the culprit?"

"Yes."

"Good. I ain't got much, but what I have I aim to keep, ya know?"

"Yes, I do. Blessings on finding another ship."

The sailor tipped his hat and headed out the door. Richard went back to the kitchen and finished clearing the counters of the various food items left out by Jorge.

Richard still couldn't believe the man had been stealing food and selling it to others. After cleaning the kitchen, he readied all the rooms, made the beds, put out fresh towels then dusted the front parlor and other areas where his guests occasionally gathered. His normal customers were overnight guests who stayed in town for a day or two. Once in a while he'd have a customer who would stay for a week.

Then there was Manny. Manny had been living in the house for the past ten years. He paid ten dollars a month, required no chambermaid, took care of his own chamber pot, which Richard had never known him to use. The man went to the outhouse more times in one night than any other person Richard had ever known. And though Richard knew he should charge Manny more than he did, he couldn't do it. The old man didn't seem to work, although at some point, Manny had apparently been a sailor. These days he was a feature at the Seaside Inn. If Manny's tales were true, he was seventy-two years old and had lived a life of adventure. He even hinted at a time or two when he might have operated as a pirate. Those stories were a little hazy.

As evening approached, he realized his schedule was shot. Richard glanced over at the ledger on his desk and decided that could wait until morning. He finally settled in for the night with a good book and tried to ignore the position he'd been put in by Jorge and Eva. In truth, he needed a wife who could help run the inn so that he could concentrate on other things, like the refurbishing of his sailboat. The thirty-two-foot, single-mast sailboat was currently in his barn having the hull scraped, sanded and repainted. His goal was to have it ready for early spring. He'd been doing most of the work. But if he had to be the one to cook and clean at the inn, he didn't see any possibility of making his timeline.

A thunderous pounding on his bedroom door rousted Richard from a deep sleep. "Coming." He scrambled out of bed, grabbed for his robe and jammed his toe on the bedpost as he tried to get to the door. Pain surged through his foot up his leg. "Great," he mumbled through gritted teeth.

He opened the door, a plastered smile on his face. "How can I help you?"

A thin man with a scar on his right cheek stood there. "Where's breakfast?"

"I'm sorry, Mr. Backus. I'll have it ready for you in a moment."

Jim Backus nodded and stepped aside. Having all male customers, Richard decided to forgo changing and went straight to the kitchen. He fired up the woodstove with small chunks so they'd burn quickly but continue to give the low heat he'd need for French toast. He grabbed one of the bottles of fresh cane syrup that he had bottled earlier in the season. He always purchased the last of the bread from the bakery at the end of the day. Today's selection of bread included a cinnamon raisin, which would make a very tasty French toast. Strawberries were in season, and they made a great garnish for the plate. Fresh-squeezed orange juice filled out the menu. Thankfully, he had sliced the bacon last night so he could put it on the other skillet.

Richard bussed the food from the kitchen to the dining area. His limp became more pronounced as his toe throbbed. He'd have to tape it. How on earth was he going to get the work done around the place with a broken toe? The men seemed to enjoy their breakfast. Grateful, he limped back into the kitchen and stopped short. "Mrs. Martin!" he gasped, and tugged his robe tighter.

"Mr. Arman, my apologies." Her face flamed. "I had an early start to my day."

"Excuse me." He stumbled back to the dining room and toward the master bedroom on the same floor.

Manny stood up as Richard passed by. "I'll take care of her."

Great! Not only had Grace Martin seen him in his robe, now Manny was going to attempt to manage the inn. Richard scurried to his room. Making certain the door was locked, he removed his robe and nightclothes, freshened up at the washbasin and dressed for the day. Unfortunately, he couldn't get his boot on over his broken toe. He put on a pair of slippers and hobbled into the kitchen, his head swimming from the pain. He found Manny and Grace washing the breakfast dishes. Grace's blond hair, spun around in a soft yellow bun, made him catch his breath and close his eyes for a moment. He counted to three then opened them…only to find the most intoxicating, compassionate pair of brown eyes. But the pain resurged, evaporating the moment.

"Mrs. Martin, I appreciate your thoughtfulness but I do not need your pity."

"Mr. Arman, Manny told me you hurt yourself, and to help you by washing some dishes seems the Christian thing to do. Don't you agree?" She placed her damp hands on her hips.

Richard turned his gaze back to the stove. He knew he was overreacting, perhaps because he had allowed his thoughts to go in the direction of how beautiful Grace was. But she was off-limits, as was any woman. "Yes, I suppose so. Please forgive me."

"If you'll allow me, I'll strip the beds that need changing and remake them with the clean linens, as well."

"I'd be a fool not to accept your help. Thank you."

"You're welcome. Now go sit down and get off your foot, or go see the doc. Either way, you should take care of it."

"I'll be fine," he mumbled. *If I keep my mind on the job and not on...*

Manny laughed. "Right, and seagulls don't eat trash. I heard you bellyaching in the kitchen this morning."

"Manny!" Richard didn't need to say more. His tone set the stage, and Manny knew to step back and keep his tongue. Well, he knew most of the time. In some ways Manny was like an eccentric old uncle.

Richard entered the dining room. Only the young sailor, Evan, remained, finishing his meal. He reached into his pocket and pulled out a silver dollar. "Here's the money for breakfast. If you don't mind, I'll be making this my home when I'm in port."

"If we have a room, I see no problem, Mr. Stanley."

"Thanks." He glanced up at the clock on the mantel. "I best be going. Thank you again for the breakfast. I won't be eating like that again for a while."

Richard chuckled. Sailors didn't have the best of diets, he knew. But Captain Jefferies, the captain Mr. Stanley would be sailing with, tended to feed his crew better than others. Richard grabbed the single slice of bacon on the table and sat down.

Grace Martin came in and gathered the rest of the dishes. "May I bring you some French toast or eggs?"

"Thank you but I can cook for myself." The pain was affecting his good manners. He reminded himself that Mrs. Martin was simply being kind.

"I am well aware that you can cook for yourself. You produced a fine fare for those men. May I be frank with you, Mr. Arman?"

Richard closed his eyes and paused. He needed to get control of his anger. Being in a bad mood for two days had not helped his well-being. But the pain in his foot made it difficult to be civil. Not to mention that he was distracted by Grace Martin's beauty. He opened his eyes and said, "Certainly."

"I understand you had a bad day yesterday, and today hasn't started off much better for you. But do you know how to accept a gift of kindness from others?"

"Pardon?"

"Here's the problem, as I see it. You're a man of pride and principles, which aren't bad characteristics, except when it comes to accepting help from another." She placed the dishes down and sat beside him. "You need to accept assistance when others offer. I went through a lot when I lost Micah. Here I was a new bride and no husband. The hardest part was, and still is, living with my parents. Once you experience independence, it's hard to sit under the control of your parents again." Grace paused. She tapped his forearm, and instant awareness of her femininity overwhelmed him. "I'll make you something to eat. Put your foot up on one of these chairs. It will help the throbbing."

"I take it you've broken a toe before?"

"Much to my chagrin, yes. Now, let me help you."

Richard nodded. He couldn't speak. He'd admired Grace Martin from afar but preferred keeping her at arm's length. In fact, he liked keeping everyone at arm's length. He'd always seen himself as a bit of an odd duck when it came to relationships. Of the few women he'd courted, no one seemed to share any similar interests. His mother said he was too particular, that there was not a perfect woman out there. But in his heart, he'd always believed there was one uniquely appointed by God to be his helpmate. That was until Willa Jean and her merciless behavior. Richard shook off those thoughts. He would not give that woman any more of his time, and that included even remembering the hurt she'd caused him.

## Chapter 2

Grace chided herself as she peeled the sheets off a guest bed. She grabbed a set of clean sheets and made up the bed. *I can't believe I was so forward, Lord. Then again, I don't like silly pretenses or biting my tongue. Father, help me find a place of my own to live.* Of course, the conversation with her parents last night didn't help her less-than-patient self. She loved her parents, she really did. But they'd been making it more difficult for her ever since she'd taken over Mercy's laundry business. They talked incessantly of suitors. A husband would be nice but…one of her own choosing would be much better.

Grace remade the bed with the fresh linens and worked her way down the hall to the next room. Seeing the bed made up and no guest's bags, she closed the door and went to the next. She repeated the process twelve times until she stumbled onto the locked door that she assumed was Manny's room.

Finished with the beds, she headed back toward the kitchen with the bundle of soiled sheets and towels. She paused at the room marked "Manager" just before she entered the kitchen and wondered if she should knock. Thinking better of it, she continued to the kitchen where Manny finished drying the last pan. "I see ya got all the laundry. You're a fast worker."

"I only found five rooms with beds that had been slept in."

"That be about right." Manny placed the frying pan in the cabinet and came up beside her. "You did a right nice thing this morning, thank you. Richard isn't a bad man, just stubborn."

Grace clamped her mouth shut and nodded. She knew better than to open her mouth and speak her mind. She'd already been too bold this morning. "You were of great help, too, this morning, Mr..." she paused. She didn't recall ever knowing or hearing Manny's last name.

"Manny," he supplied.

"Well, Manny, I must be off. I have other customers waiting on me."

Manny stepped back half a step and let her pass. At the door she turned and said, "Let Mr. Arman know that I'll return early in the morning to fix breakfast for the men."

Manny smiled, a toothless wonder grinning back at her.

The small horse-drawn wagon she'd brought this morning sat in the backyard of the inn. Her horse was busily munching on the flower bed. "Jasper, stop that." Grace plopped the linens in the back of the wagon and pulled Jasper away from the tasty treats.

The backyard of the Seaside Inn was large enough to hang all the sheets. A small but ample garden, a paved patio and a large barn filled out the rest of the yard.

She turned back and led Jasper out of the yard backward, set his bridle back in place and mounted the small wagon. She gathered the reins and headed south to The Conch, one of her few remaining customers. She hoped and prayed the proprietor would not be upset with her being late.

"Good morning, Mr. Learner. How are you today?" she greeted him cheerily a few minutes later.

"Fine. You're running a little late."

"I'm afraid I am. Forgive me."

"Nothing to forgive, child."

Grace pulled over the wagon and grabbed the clean bundle of Mr. Learner's laundry.

Mr. Learner handed over a white laundry bag filled with soiled linens. Grace took the proffered bag and handed him the bag with the clean ones.

"It's a pleasure to see you this morning, Mrs. Martin. I'll see you in the morning, perhaps on time?"

"Wait, Mr. Learner. I'm afraid I'll be late again tomorrow. Mr. Arman broke a toe, and I offered to chamber his rooms for a couple of days. I hope you don't mind."

Mr. Learner, with his white-and gray-speckled beard smiled. "No, child. That's a right neighborly thing to do. I'll expect you an hour later until you tell me otherwise."

"Thank you for understanding, Mr. Learner."

He smiled again and stepped back inside his inn. The Conch had no more than three or four guest rooms, and Mr. Learner, well into his seventies, handled the place quite ably. Mrs. Learner was not fairing quite as well. It had been ages since she had seen Mrs. Learner out and about.

Grace loaded the wagon and headed home. She'd rather stay in town and mingle with folks than go home to face her nagging parents. It just seemed she could do nothing to their satisfaction anymore. Grace sighed. Her shoulders slumped. She gathered the reins and signaled for Jasper to take them home. If only...

Richard couldn't believe how much pain one little toe could cause the body. He knew better than to go see the doctor since there was nothing he could do for a broken toe. But he was reconsidering, thinking maybe he should visit him to get something for the pain. Unfortunately, Mrs. Martin was right; keeping the foot elevated was the best treatment for the pain and swelling. He just couldn't afford the time. He needed to get some work done. The better part of wisdom was to discover just how much his employees had taken from him. He drove to the market to settle his accounts, his foot swollen and throbbing. He jumped down from his buggy and instantly regretted it.

"Hey there, Mr. Arman, need a hand?" George Leonardy, the local butcher, asked. "Broke a toe. I'm fine. I came to settle my accounts."

George sobered. "I am glad, Mr. Arman. I was about to speak with you. Jorge has run up a high tab."

Richard felt the weight of the world slam down on his shoulders. He should have been more vigilant. "When did he charge last?"

"Yesterday. He picked up a side of beef. Forgive me for asking, but where would you keep such a large piece of meat."

"I didn't order it."

"Ahh... So then, Jorge does not have the authority to order more meat from your account?"

"No, sir, he does not. I'm afraid we'll need to get the

sheriff involved." Richard shuffled most of his weight onto his left foot.

"I understand. I'll be happy to get Sheriff Bower. I'm sorry but…"

Richard raised his hand. "I should have realized sooner when my food bill went up last week. I'll settle my accounts. However, can we work out something with regard to yesterday's purchase?"

"Yes, Mr. Arman. I would not like to lose you as a customer. I can sell you the side of beef at the cost I paid for it."

"Thank you. You are most kind, Mr. Leonardy."

George smiled. "As I said, you are a good customer, as was your grandmother before you. Give me a couple of minutes to get the sheriff. Go inside and find a seat."

Richard nodded and hobbled into the butcher shop. Inside he found George's wife, Ignacia, working behind the counter.

"Good morning, Mr. Arman. Your inn must be full, no?"

"You must be thinking of the side of beef. No, the inn is not full. Jorge stole from me and from you."

Ignacia paled.

Richard raised his hands. "Do not worry. I will cover Jorge's purchase. I should have sent a messenger to all of my suppliers yesterday."

"What happened?"

"Jorge is a thief. He was using my money to line his own pockets. He was purchasing food on my account then preparing and selling it to people behind my back."

Ignacia shook her head. "I am so sorry to hear such bad things about Jorge. He was always nice to George and me. George should be inside in a moment. He was sweeping the sidewalk."

"He went to Sheriff Bower's office for me."

"Ah. What can I get you?"

"I'm here to settle my accounts with George. But if it is not too much to ask, may I sit down and get the weight off my foot?"

"Of course, forgive me. Come back inside to our home."

"Thank you." Richard followed Ignacia back to a small room, and he sat down on the sofa. She pushed a hassock over to rest his foot on. "I will send in Sheriff Bower and George when they arrive."

"Thank you, Mrs. Leonardy."

"You're welcome, Mr. Arman. I am sorry for your troubles. Hopefully, the sheriff can settle the matter."

Ignacia went back into the store area and left him in their private room. He relieved the pressure on his foot and enjoyed the hassock's comfort. It was a quaint room, modestly furnished but comfortable. His thoughts drifted back to what Mr. Leonardy said of Jorge's purchase. If Jorge had charged an entire side of beef to the Seaside Inn account at the butcher shop, there would be no telling what else he had charged in other shops. The grocer would be the next stop. Perhaps he could convince the sheriff to go with him. Speaking of...

The sheriff loomed in the doorway. "Mr. Leonardy says a former employee has stolen from you?"

Richard started to rise. "Sit. George told me about your broken toe."

Richard glanced down at his throbbing foot. "Thank you. Yes, it appears that Jorge has been stealing for a while now. He was preparing meals at the inn then selling them, making quite a profit for himself and robbing me blind. It's my own fault. I noticed the bills were getting higher, but I ignored them for a month, possibly two. I fired him yesterday morning. He came by here and ordered a side of beef on my tab. Is there anything we can do?"

"Theft is theft, and while it would be hard to prove he was selling meals out of the inn, this side of beef... that is much easier. Were there any witnesses to the time you fired him?"

"Yes, Grace Martin was in the alley when I fired both Jorge and my chambermaid, Eva. I believe Eva may have been sharing in the profits with Jorge, but I do not know this to be the case."

The sheriff nodded. "I think we can get back the beef or at least the money Jorge is making from the sale of it. In either case, are you willing to press charges against Jorge?"

"I guess I am. I need to go to my other suppliers and make certain he hasn't run up bills with them, as well."

"I'll be happy to travel with you and settle this matter quickly."

George walked in with a folded slip of white paper in his hands. "I'm sorry, Mr. Arman. I will not allow anyone to charge on your account from now on."

"It's probably best. It will put a restraint on my time, but I fear it cannot be avoided."

George nodded. "I put the actual cost I was charged for the beef as well as my discounted price. This way the sheriff knows just how much has been stolen from you." George handed the paper over to Richard.

Richard scanned the figures. His eyes widened. A thin bead of sweat started to form on his forehead. "I'll have this settled by the end of the week."

George nodded and went back into the storefront.

"How bad?"

Richard handed the bill to Sheriff Bower. "I generally spend twenty to twenty five dollars a month here."

The sheriff rolled back on his heels. "A hundred and fifty dollars! And that's taking his discount off the full price of the beef. We'd best find Mr. Jorge Salvador pronto. Where else has he been authorized to charge for your inn?"

"The grocer's. I don't believe he could charge on my behalf anywhere else. Oh, wait…the fish market." Richard's stomach turned. *Dear Lord, how much has he stolen from me?*

Grace wiped her hands on a dry towel after scouring the pot clean. The laundry flapped in the breeze. In a few hours, she'd begin gathering the sheets and folding them for her customers. For now she needed to work on her household chores. She entered her home and enjoyed the breeze blowing through the front and back doors, east to west. Cracker houses were all the rage because they were built to help cool the indoors from the high summer temps. A wraparound porch shaded all of the downstairs windows, as well as the center of the house from the front door to the rear. The house was totally devoid of impairments for the wind to blow through.

"Grace," her mother called out from the kitchen. "Would you come in here, please?"

Grace took in a deep pull of air and released it slowly. The one conversation she had been hoping to avoid was the one she felt certain her mother would bring up. Grace stepped toward the kitchen. "What can I do for you, Mother?"

"Nothing, sit." She patted the stool next to her. "I realize we haven't had much time to simply chat with one another in what seems like ages."

Grace sat and allowed a slight smile to form on her lips.

"I received a letter from Mercy," Grace offered to get the conversation going on something other than herself. "Mercy's expecting their first child."

"Oh, that's sweet. Rosemarie must be beside herself. This will be her third grandchild."

"Fourth. Jackson Jr. and his wife are expecting, as well."

"Oh my, their quiver is filling up." Grace's spine stiffened. Her mother's desire to have grandchildren was palpable. It wasn't that Grace didn't want to be a mother. It just didn't feel right to marry after losing Micah.

"Well, my goodness, look at the time. Would you mind helping me shell the peas?"

"I'd be happy to. Do we have anything else coming out of the garden?"

"Oh my, yes. I'll be canning for hours over the next few weeks. Your father is experimenting with more drying. He's leaving the beans on the stalks and letting the sun dry the seeds in the pods."

"What about insects?"

"He's experimenting with various oils and soaps. We shall see." Helen Flowers, Grace's mother, was a woman content to let her husband do whatever he saw fit, unlike her good friend, Mercy's mother, Rosemarie Hastings. Grace had never seen or heard her mother question her father about the decisions he'd made. Which left Grace feeling like she didn't have an ally in her mother. "Grace, I know your father wants what is best for you…"

Grace sighed.

"I'm sorry." Her mother apologized and didn't say another word.

"Mother, I know he wants what is best for me. But I'm not ready. I still love Micah. I don't know if I'll ever be ready."

"Ready or not, you'll be marrying someone by the end of the summer," her father huffed, stepping unexpectedly into the kitchen. "You've got a month to pick someone. After that, I'll choose." Grace balled her fists.

## Chapter 3

Exhausted after a day of discovering just how deep in debt he was, thanks to Jorge, Richard unhitched his horse from the buggy and limped his way into the horse's stall. He had found Brownie, a Belgian draft horse, alone and hungry in the woods pulling what was left of a broken wagon. Richard had nursed the poor animal back to health. "Looks like I'm in need of some of my own nursing skills, boy." He stroked Brownie's neck.

He took care of the horse's needs, set out some fresh oats then made his way back to the house. He'd planned on being out for only an hour. Instead, he'd been gone for four. Jorge was nowhere to be found, but Sheriff Bower would continue the search. He washed his hands and face and went to his room where he could do his paperwork.

Sitting down, he strained and pulled until he finally got the boot off his swollen foot. His foot was killing him. He'd tried to elevate it as often as possible, but there weren't enough hours in the day.

Sitting down at his desk, he reluctantly started working on the books. He would be dipping into his savings to cover the expenses he had incurred from Jorge's thievery. Unfortunately, only Mr. Leonardy had reduced the price to his actual costs.

The bell over the front door jangled. Richard shuffled toward the front desk. "Welcome to the Seaside Inn. My name is Richard Arman. How may I help you?"

A middle-aged man stepped forward, while his wife and two children remained at the front door. "We're looking for a room."

Richard scanned the cut of the man's clothes. They were neat and well tailored but also well used. No seams were fraying but... He glanced down at the man's shoes. Shoes always told the truth of a man's financial standing. "Our rooms only have one bed in them. I could put a cot in one of the rooms."

"We will be fine with a single room."

"Very well. The cost of the room is one dollar per night. How many nights will you be staying?"

"Just the one. We are traveling."

"We offer a breakfast for a dollar per person but I'd be happy to give all four of you a break and offer it for two dollars for the entire family." A hint of a sparkle caught the wife's eyes.

"That would be wonderful, thank you."

"Sign here, please." Richard pointed to the line in the register. "Can I help with your bags?"

"Thank you, no, we'll manage."

"Very well. You'll be in room four at the top of the

stairs. Turn right and it will be the last door on your right. There's a lovely view of the harbor from your room."

"Thank you." The man scribbled his name.

Richard grabbed the key from the cubby and placed it on the counter. He glanced at the register. "Welcome to the Seaside Inn, Mr. Robbins, Mrs. Robbins."

The gentleman pulled three dollars out of his billfold and passed them over to Richard. "Call me John. Most folks do."

"All right then, make yourselves at home. There's a common room with a library to my left, and the dining room is off to the right where we serve breakfast from six to eight o'clock."

"That will suit our needs quite well, thank you."

John Robbins gathered his family like a small flock of geese and herded them up the stairs.

"I'll bring fresh water up in a few minutes."

Climbing the stairs was not something he was looking forward to doing. He should have put the family in a downstairs room. But in truth, he'd given them the largest room so they wouldn't feel too crowded. Richard scanned the street in front of the inn. A team of older horses sat with a wagon chock full of the family's belongings. Obviously, they had fallen on bad times. And with the recent development that placed him in debt, there was little he could offer the family.

*Lord, help me get out from under this debt as soon as possible,* he silently prayed.

He had the funds to cover the debt, but those funds had been set aside for other things, like remodeling his sailboat and savings for some repairs he figured would be needed for the inn in the next couple of years. And with all the talk of indoor plumbing, he knew he'd have to put in a modern bathroom or two and lose a couple of rooms in the process.

Saving was imperative if he was going to keep this business afloat for as many years as his grandmother hoped. And in truth, he liked the business. He enjoyed meeting new people and serving them. The problem came in finding good help. Help he could rely upon, unlike Jorge and Eva. He knew he needed to get beyond his anger toward them, but that was going to take a while.

The bell above the door jangled again. Richard looked up and noticed a man ducking below the door header. He was young and tall, taller than anyone he'd ever seen. Within five minutes Whit Majors was registered and going down the hall to his room. The bell rang again. If this kept up, he'd have the entire place rented out for the evening, which would be wonderful considering the debt he needed to clear up.

While he didn't rent every room, he was busy, too busy to finish his bookwork. By the end of the day, his foot throbbed. His frustration with Jorge and not being able to figure out a plan that would solve his problem without dipping into his savings bothered him enough that his nightly prayers were laced with frustration. "Father, forgive my sour disposition. Help me trust in Your provisions for my life."

Richard crawled into bed. The purple and red swelling around his toe told the story. He'd started the day off wrong and it hadn't ended much better, but he was trying to see a positive in all the negatives.

Fortunately, the next morning was not a repeat of the day before. Mrs. Martin's help with the breakfast was a godsend. She arrived just as the first of the boarders came to the breakfast table. Pancakes with fresh whipped cream, chocolate sauce and some bananas were a part of the menu. The hearty aromas from the kitchen and on the table enticed him to eat more than he should. He had a rare treat this morning sitting and enjoying the company of his boarders, all because of the generosity of Mrs. Martin. The incredible woman warmed him with a smile that was liquid sunshine. She also seemed to put the sailors on their best behavior. Then there were the Robbins children, alive with giggles and laughter. The sailors ate with gusto, and most had second helpings. It seemed that even Manny stopped talking long enough to eat two plates full. And though they went through three pounds of bacon and a couple pounds of sausages, the pancakes helped fill the bellies and lower his food expenses. He paused for a moment, wondering if he should ask Mrs. Martin if she would like to work for him. He thought better of it and went to his desk.

Richard began working on the numbers he'd been unable to do yesterday. A few more nights of nearly full capacity would bring his savings back with an even greater speed. But it wasn't fair not to pay Grace Martin for all the extra work she'd been doing. *Would* she be interested in working for him? Again Richard mulled the idea around for a bit.

"Richard!" Manny hollered at full voice.

One day it would be nice to not have his name called out in such a manner. Of course, that would mean the end of Manny's presence, and Richard found comfort in the old man, as odd a character as he was. "Be right there," he called back.

Richard came into the kitchen and didn't see him there, so he entered the dining room. Still no Manny. He went to the front desk where he found the Robbins family with Manny behind the desk. "These folks were wondering if they could stay another night," Manny supplied, grinning like a Halloween pumpkin.

"Certainly," Richard answered, and moved behind the counter. "Where are you traveling to, Mr. Robbins?"

"Georgia. My father has a spot of land he said we could stay on. I'll need to find a job, but Elaine and the kids will have a roof over their heads."

"I take it ya hit a bad spell?" Manny inquired.

Richard glared at him.

"Yes," John whispered. "I lost a small ranch. I tried to raise cattle, but I couldn't keep up with the feed."

"Same deal as before? One room, four breakfasts?"

"Yes, but I'll pay full price on the breakfast. The kids ate just as much as the others."

Richard smiled. "I tell you what. If your wife wouldn't mind helping strip the beds and making up fresh ones, I'll feed you for free in the morning."

John turned to his wife. She beamed. "I'd be happy to."

"Wonderful. Mrs. Martin—she's in the kitchen—will show you where the clean linens are kept. Rooms two, three and eleven paid for a couple nights so you won't need to change their linens. And the same goes for your room, as well."

"Thank you, Mr. Arman. God bless you." Elaine Robbins smiled then ran off to the kitchen.

John extended his hand. "Thank you, sir."

"Pleasure is all mine."

The bell over the door rang. Sheriff Bower came in, removing his hat. "Good morning, Mr. Arman."

"Good morning, Sheriff. Any luck tracking down the individual?"

"Yes, sir. I'd like to speak with you about that, however. Are you selling breakfast this morning?"

"They have pancakes," answered the youngest Robbins, a little girl with golden ringlets that bounced when she spoke.

"Well then, if you're still serving, I could use some pancakes."

"And sausage and bacon and eggs and some sort of fancy potatoes. They were really good. I ate too much." The Robbins boy rubbed his tummy.

Richard chuckled. "Can't get a better recommendation than that."

"No, sir, I don't believe I could." The sheriff pulled out a silver dollar. "Here ya go. I'll set myself down in the dining room."

"I'll join ya, Sheriff," Manny said as he waddled behind.

About twenty minutes later, Richard was able to sequester himself and the sheriff in the front parlor. "Am I to take it you found Jorge?"

"Yes, and he gave me this." The sheriff pulled out a wad of rolled up paper bills about an inch and a half thick. "He's wondering if you would drop the charges if he paid you back for all he's taken from you."

"I don't know, Sheriff." Richard took the cash and began to unroll the bills.

"There's a hundred there."

"He owes me more like three hundred."

"Ah." The sheriff leaned back in his chair and placed his right foot on top of his left knee.

"If he pays his way out of the crime, will he be inclined to do it again to someone else?"

"Probably. But I don't know. I did, however, put the

fear of God into him. I reminded him how easy it was for me to find him and how easy it was to prove he was guilty of theft. I also told him it was not unheard of for a man to lose his hand if he continues to steal." The sheriff leaned forward and added in a whisper, "Not in this country… but I didn't tell him that." He sat back again with a self-satisfied smile. "Honestly, I don't know if he has a history of this kind of behavior or not. And perhaps he's a smooth enough talker that he pays restitution and moves on from one place to another. It's up to you, Richard."

"Can I take a day or two to think on the matter?"

"Absolutely. I'll keep him in the holding cell for a couple of days. It will do him some good."

The sheriff glanced toward the front door and toward the Robbins's family wagon. "Who's this family packed to the gills out there?"

"John Robbins. I'm not sure where he hails from, but he had a cattle ranch and lost it. He's heading back toward his father's in Georgia."

"Hmm. You know, Jackson Hastings might be looking for another hand. With his son Ben going off to college to be a medical doctor and all, he might just be ready to hire."

"I'll mention it to Mr. Robbins." Richard stood. "Thank you, Sheriff." He offered his hand.

The sheriff took it. "You're welcome. I wish all my cases were this easy."

Sheriff Bower left, and Grace Martin walked into the room. Richard silently cleared his throat. He needed to distract himself from her beauty and concentrate on her benevolent spirit and possible friendship. "I set Mrs. Robbins up with the rooms and linens."

"Thank you." Richard rose and headed toward the front desk.

"That's a mighty generous offer, especially in light of what happened with Jorge and Eva."

"Perhaps. I want to pay you for the work you've been doing and hire you to work for the next couple of weeks, if that is agreeable to you. But I reckon you're probably too busy with your laundry business."

"Actually, I'm not too busy. I've lost a few customers lately. It's all very odd. They say they're happy with my work but then turn around and hire another laundress. I know I'm not charging more than others."

"So, working for me would be good for both of us?" He was pleased that he would be a blessing to her as well as she being a blessing to him and the inn.

"Yes, thank you, Mr. Arman."

"No. Thank you."

Grace smiled and gave a nod. "I'll return in a half hour for the soiled linens."

"Very well, thank you. What do you want for a salary?"

"Oh, I don't know. Whatever you paid Eva or Jorge is fine."

Richard nodded. He hobbled back to his room. The roll of a hundred dollars in his pocket weighed more like a hundred pounds. The fate of Jorge was in his hands.

Grace found she enjoyed helping Richard Arman with breakfast. There was a peace working here with him. A peace she no longer felt in her parents' home. Her father's proclamation that if she didn't choose someone to court within a month... Grace stopped the train of thoughts. She wouldn't lose another moment's peace of mind over her father's ridiculous demands. Instead her mind drifted over to Richard Arman. She found herself curious about the man. For the past couple of months their relationship was that of a customer and server. Now she found herself with the unique opportunity to see him operate up close and personal. From what she witnessed, Jorge and Eva were in the wrong, not Richard Arman. He seemed to be generous to a fault. She spent the morning mulling over these new insights into Richard Arman while she washed the linens of her two remaining clients.

"Grace," her mother called out, "would you mind doing my laundry, as well?"

"I'll take care of it," Grace answered, then reloaded the washing pot over the fire. Inside the house, she pulled the soiled linens from their baskets and brought them out to the washbasin. Oddly enough, ever since she'd started working for Mercy and then took over the laundry business, her mother hadn't done any of the family's laundry. And yet her parents complained that she wasn't getting enough chores done. If only she could find an affordable place to live. In spite of her father's protests, she was old enough to live on her own. She could even procure her own establishment. After all, she was a widow, and that gave her some rights, didn't it?

A small buggy pulled up to the back fence. A woman dressed in a gay outfit stood up and called out, "Grace."

"Hope? Is that you?" Hope's crimson hair was always a giveaway. "What are you all dressed up for?" Hope was a couple of years younger than Grace, but they found in each other someone they could talk with. Grace put down the wet clothes, dried off her hands and headed over to the fence.

"I'm venturing out and hoping to get a job at one of

the hotels, or some place. I can take orders. I'm pretty good with figures. I want to do something with my life, like you and Mercy. However, I don't want to wash other people's laundry. I do it because it is a necessary chore, but I don't like it. And I especially don't like what it does to my hands."

"You do have sensitive skin."

"You've got that right. What would be wonderful is to marry a man who can hire someone to do the laundry and all the other chores I'm not too fond of."

Grace chuckled. "Chores are a part of life."

"Oh, I know. But a girl can dream, can't she?"

"Of course." Grace winked. "Where'd you get that outfit?"

"I made it. Isn't it splendid?" Hope stood up in the buggy and gave a quarter spin in one direction then a quarter spin in the other, giving Grace the full view of the outfit.

Grace eyed the design and seams. It was more modern than anything she'd ever seen, even in those French and English magazines. "Very handsome lines."

"Thank you. I believe it will be more practical for business. Too many layers would get in the way of moving quickly in an office. And I cut down the bustle to little more than a slight bump. And I love rich purples and dark green, and black also goes so well with it. But of course a white blouse just sets it off perfectly with the slight ribbon of color around the collar and cuffs. Don't you agree?"

It was a sharp-looking outfit. "It seems practical. Have you thought about dressmaking as a business?"

"Yes…well…no. I don't believe I'm ready to have a business of my own. There's so much more than simply going to work and putting in your hours."

Grace held back her laughter. Hope's father was an investor, and Hope was often asked to help analyze businesses. She had a quick mind for figures, but her father's clients weren't accepting of women's opinions. "Yes, I know."

Hope sucked in a gasp of air. "Oh, goodness, I didn't mean... Oh, I don't know what I mean. Fiddlesticks." Hope plopped back down in her buggy.

"It's all right, Hope. I'm not offended."

"Oh, good. Then wish me well. I am off to conquer the world." Hope picked up the reins and headed down the street.

"Dear Lord, protect her." Grace went back to her mother's laundry and finished hanging the clothing in time to remove the dried towels from the line.

She woke before the sun rose the next morning, grateful that her parents hadn't continued with their demands that she quit her laundry business. Of course, from time to time she often thought about quitting. But if she was to ever get out from under her parents' roof, quitting wasn't an option. On the other hand, if things went well working for Richard Arman, perhaps another job would work and provide the needed funds. *Lord, You know my prayers and my needs. Please help me.*

She drove on to the Seaside Inn, continuing her prayers and trying to figure out a way to be on her own.

As the sun rose over the horizon, Grace pulled the buggy into the rear yard of the inn and parked. She ran inside to wash her hands and get ready for the morning breakfast run. Today she planned on making a similar fare as she had prepared the day before, with one exception. She was going to make a Spanish-style potato casserole. She brought in one jalapeño pepper from her garden to add a bit of heat to the dish. Not too much, and she'd be careful not to include the seeds, which were the hottest part of the pepper, but just enough to give a little zip to the morning meal.

She pulled the white apron off the hook and turned. "Father? What are you doing here?"

Richard Arman stood behind him, shaking his head. Her father paled.

"Father?"

# Chapter 4

Henry Flowers wavered a moment at the appearance of his daughter then steadied himself. "What are you doing here?" he bellowed.

"I work here."

Her father turned and faced Richard Arman. "You hired my daughter?"

"Yes, sir. She's a fine cook and an excellent help."

"Well," Henry Flowers blustered, "you'll do as I say, you understand me?"

Richard squared his shoulders and leaned into her father. Without raising his voice, he spoke in a very firm tone, "You, sir, are out of line and no longer welcome in my establishment." Richard pivoted his body and extended his arm toward the door.

Henry Flowers turned back to his daughter. "You'll heed my warning and leave this position right away. I shall have a proper suitor for you when you return home this evening."

"No, Father. You said I had a month. I will not…" Grace let her words trail off. "We'll discuss this at home, privately." She went over to the stove and pulled out the cast-iron frying pan. There would be no casserole this morning. She didn't have the focus to watch the dish carefully. Instead she'd make some muffins and hash browns.

She refused to look at her father and listened to his footfalls as he stomped out of the room. A cock crowed from somewhere down the street. Grace's hands shook as she tried to cut the potatoes.

Richard came up beside her. "I'm sorry you had to go through that."

"What did he want?"

"He was trying to convince me to fire you from your laundry business. He said you needed to get married but no man wanted to pursue a woman who…"

Grace's mind zipped through all the conversations she'd been having with her father and mother about her job. Was he behind her loss of customers? "I'm sorry my father put you in such a position, Mr. Arman. If you wish, I can…"

He cut her off. "Hush. You heard my words to your father. You are a good worker, and I couldn't have done half as well as you did with yesterday's breakfast."

The rapid footfalls coming down the stairs broke the ability to speak further. "We'll discuss this later. But I'd say the Robbins children are ready for their breakfast."

Grace gave him a halfhearted smile and went back to work. In one pan she started frying up some bacon. And in another she began cooking up some eggs. In fifteen minutes she had eggs, bacon, sausage and hash-brown potatoes ready. Muffins just about done in the oven, she prepared the batter for blueberry pancakes. As an after-thought, she started making blueberry syrup from scratch for the pancakes.

Breakfast went as well as the day before. As things calmed down, Grace started to put together the Span-ish potato casserole for the next day. She could heat up smaller portions tomorrow…if she still had a job. More important, if she still had a home. Given her father's cur-rent attitude, he might just have reached his limit of her standing up to him. Not that she hadn't reached her limit of his trying to control and run her life. There had to be a way to make matters better between them, but how?

"Mrs. Martin!" The Robbins girl came bursting into the kitchen. "That was scrummy. Thank you for the blue-berry pancakes."

"You're welcome, miss."

"Momma said she would make them once we have a home." Her lips were stained purplish-blue from the blueberry syrup.

Grace's heart went out to the little girl. "What's your name, sweetheart?"

"Lillie."

Grace wiped her hands on a cloth and knelt down on one knee. "That's a pretty name. I'm glad you liked my pancakes." If anyone could empathize with what a per-son goes through without a home, Grace could.

"They were delicious but I loved the blueberry syrup."

"I can tell. You'll need to wash your face again this morning. You have blue lips."

Lillie stuck out her tongue and mumbled, "Is my tongue blue, too?"

Grace chuckled. "Yes." She stood up and went back

to the sink. "I have to get back to work. Have a good day, Lillie."

"Oh, I will. Daddy's going to see a cattle rancher about a job. Momma doesn't want to go to Georgia and live on Grandpa's land. She likes Grandpa, but she said the land has too many attachments."

Grace could relate.

She finished her work for Richard Arman and continued on to The Conch. Mr. Learner stood on the outside step and waved. "Good morning, Mrs. Martin."

"Good morning, Mr. Learner. How is Mrs. Learner this morning?"

"Better, thank you." He stepped down, glanced to the right and left then leaned in. "Your father was here this morning. He's strongly suggesting that I switch to a different laundry service."

Grace rolled her eyes. "What did you say?"

"Not what your father wanted to hear. I understand his concern, but I disagree with his methods. Do you wish to remarry, Mrs. Martin?"

"Someday, perhaps. But I won't marry simply for the sake of marriage. I'm hoping to rent a room and live on my own soon. You are not the only customer my father has been speaking to." Grace was more and more convinced that her father's meddling was responsible for her current lack of customers. "My problem is finding a place to rent that has room to do my business. A fair amount of property is needed to dry all that laundry."

"Which is why I employ your services. The missus and I will be praying for you. Perhaps you can reason with your father."

Grace moaned. She'd been arguing with him constantly, and today when she arrived home, it would be an all-out shouting match, of that she was certain. Because no matter whom her father set up for her to marry, she would not marry him.

Mr. Learner handed her the small bundle of linens. Grace retrieved the clean stack. "Shall I put these in the linen closet for you?"

"No, thank you." He handed her a small brown envelope. "Here's this week's payment. I hope you'll be able to live peacefully with your father."

"Thank you, Mr. Learner."

He placed a loving hand on her shoulder. "Your job is secure here. Thank you, and Godspeed, Grace."

His hand slipped off her shoulder, and he eased his old frame back up the stairs. Grace offered a quick prayer for Mr. and Mrs. Learner and their health.

She grabbed the reins and headed back toward home. The weight of the impending argument sagged on her shoulders. Perhaps she should pack her belongings, take what little money she had saved and flee to Massachusetts and her friend Mercy Darling.

Richard couldn't believe the impertinence of Mr. Flowers coming and demanding that he stop using Grace's laundry service. And only because he couldn't convince anyone to take his daughter as a wife because she was far too independent. The woman was a jewel. And if a man couldn't see that, he had no right even considering asking Grace Martin for her hand in marriage. Which he would have said to Mr. Flowers if he felt the man would have listened. Over the years he'd dealt with men like him and knew that the better part of wisdom was to not engage in frivolous conversation. Not that Mrs. Martin's matrimonial state was frivolous, but that he had no right to interfere on her behalf, apart from telling Mr. Flowers he wouldn't be taking his advice.

The bell above the door jangled. Sheriff Bower walked in. "Good morning, Mr. Arman. Have you made a decision regarding Jorge?"

"I'm still considering it. I suppose you want an answer as soon as possible."

"Yes, sir. I can't hold him much longer without charging him. However, you should know that I have searched some reports and found someone matching Jorge's description using another name doing much the same kind of crime. I've wired for additional information from the sheriff in that area but haven't heard back yet."

"As much as I don't want to, I fear I must go forward with the charges against him. Not for my sake as much as for the protection of others. Jorge—or whatever his name is—must face the consequences of his actions."

"I'll draw up the necessary papers, and you can come in and sign them."

"I'll come to your office shortly after one. Will that be sufficient?"

The sheriff put on his hat and gave an affirmative nod, then paused as he made his way out the door. "For what it is worth, I believe you are making the right decision. Jorge does not appear to be remorseful, only frustrated that he was caught. Good day, Mr. Arman."

"Good day, Sheriff." Richard limped back to his room and removed his shoe. The broken toe throbbed. He needed some ice. He walked on his right heel so as not to put pressure on the toe and headed toward the kitchen.

"Whoa, that looks painful." Manny whistled.

"It is." Richard bent down and opened the icebox. Inside he found a variety of items he didn't recall purchasing. "Manny, did you pick up some items for breakfast?"

"Nope. Must have been Mrs. Martin. She's a sweet one, that one, and golly, she can cook."

Richard smiled, his belly still full from breakfast. "Yes, she can."

"Not that your meals aren't fine," Manny stumbled.

"I know what you mean. She adds just a little extra to the plate, like that blueberry syrup this morning." He glanced over the counter. "What's that?"

"A Spanish potato casserole for tomorrow's breakfast. After it cools I'm supposed to put it in the icebox." Manny paused. "You know, you ought to marry that one. She's a keeper."

Richard let out a nervous chuckle. "I'm not the marrying kind."

"You look like the marrying kind to me. Then again, I'm not the marrying kind, either. If I was thirty years younger, I might be reconsidering. Mrs. Martin is a mighty fine catch, I tell ya." Manny popped a muffin into his mouth and headed for the back door. "I've got some errands in town. Can I get you anything?"

"No, thank you. You've done quite enough." Images of Grace Martin as his wife danced through his mind. She would make an excellent wife, even an excellent innkeeper's wife. But Richard knew better than to consider bringing another woman into his life. The past had taught him all too well that he was not fit for marriage. He didn't have the patience any longer. And marriage took patience, as best he could tell.

He chipped a small chunk off the ice block and grabbed a small towel. The ice would reduce the swelling. Then he must get to town and finish his errands—first the bank then on to his suppliers. A visit to the sheriff's office and signing the charges against Jorge would be the final stop. He walked back to his room and placed the ice on his toe. He winced and held it there. If he didn't get the swelling down, he wouldn't be able to do any of his errands. Feeling agitated, he reached for his Bible and started to read. Perhaps the Lord could calm his unsettled spirit. He closed his eyes and prayed for Mrs. Martin, her father and the entire situation. Again he saw her living in the inn as his wife. *Dear Lord, help me get Manny's foolish suggestion out of my mind.*

"Grace!" Her father came up beside her.

She stood at the kitchen sink and turned her back to him. "I am not ready to discuss this with you, Father. Please leave me be."

"Don't you understand it is time for you to get on with your life and get married again?"

She fought back the desire to engage her father in battle. She knew that if she was to open her mouth, ugly words would pass, and as of this moment she couldn't control her anger. She knew he meant well, and she loved him. He was just so overbearing sometimes, and she was tired of his constant manipulations. She was no longer a child, and he didn't have the right to order her about as if she were.

"Very well. Expect David Ferris to be here at five o'clock to engage in conversation. He would like to meet you."

Grace turned and faced him. She balled her fists and counted one…two…three… She breathed in deeply and let it out slowly. Four…five…. "Please convey my regrets to Mr. Ferris. I will not be seeing guests this evening. I do not know this man. And even if he were to be a potential suitor, my anger with you is so high at the moment, I would not be gracious to him." Grace paused, considering what she was about to say next. "You must understand you have forced me to make this decision. If I am a burden to you and Mother, I shall leave."

He paled, then an instant flush of crimson stained his cheeks. "You will follow my orders," he said through clenched teeth, his entire body trembling with rage.

Grace remained calm. "No, I will not. I am a grown woman and I am a widow, something you yourself have not experienced. While there is a lot more of life for me to learn, I am an adult, and I shall not stay under your roof for a moment longer. I will pack my belongings, and I'll be gone in the morning." She turned and walked away.

"Grace Flowers, you get back here!"

She stopped and faced him once again. "That's Mrs. Martin to you, sir." Again she turned and held back the tears. Her heart was breaking. She loved her father, but she had reached her limit. For the past year the increase of tension between the two of them had been bubbling to the surface, and now it had overflowed. She went up the stairs to her room and started to pack. After thirty minutes she had most of her clothing sorted.

She lifted the lid of her hope chest at the foot of the bed. Inside were a few special items from her wedding she'd held on to. She removed the picture of Micah from her dresser and put it on top of a white-linen tablecloth sewn together by his great-grandmother and given to him at the time of their wedding. Gliding her hand against the soft fabric, she remembered Micah's eyes when they opened the gift. It was a family heirloom and an honor. She should give it back to the Martins, she reflected, closing the lid. They should pass it down to another in the family.

"Grace Ann, it's me, Mother. Please open the door."

"There's nothing left to say, Mother."

"Please try and understand...."

Grace sighed, walked over to the door and opened it. "I can't be manipulated any longer. He does not respect me or my choices."

"Please reconsider. Mr. Ferris is a nice man."

"I'm sure he is, but this isn't only about Mr. Ferris. Father went to my clients and persuaded them to not hire me."

"No, your father wouldn't do that," Helen protested.

Grace snickered. "I caught him this morning speaking with Mr. Arman at the Seaside Inn. He also had been to see Mr. Learner at The Conch. You cannot defend him for these actions."

Her mother clamped her mouth shut.

"Mother, I love you. I shall always love you. I even love Father. But I do not like him at the moment. Give me some time. Perhaps in a while I will come and visit, but for now I must leave."

"Where will you go?"

"I'll rent a room somewhere. Perhaps I can work for my rent. I don't know. But I cannot live under Father's roof a moment longer. I am not his little girl to be ordered about like a slave. I am a grown woman, and I alone am responsible for my decisions. Good or bad, they are my choices to make."

Her mother reached out to her and placed a loving hand on her shoulder. "Promise me you will call on me if you are in need."

"I will try." At the moment she couldn't see coming to her parents for any need. Her father would have more strings attached and an attitude so thick it would be hard to breathe.

Her mother enveloped her in an embrace and hugged her with all the strength she possessed. Tears filled Grace's eyes and started to tumble down her cheeks. She pulled away. "I need to get back to work."

"What of your belongings in the parlor?"

There were a few chairs and a table that Micah had built. "I will call for them when I have a permanent home."

Helen dabbed her eyes with a handkerchief. "I love you."

"I love you, too, Mother." Grace embraced her mother. She hated to hurt her but Father had left her no choice.

Grace continued to pack late into the evening, avoiding dinner with her parents. After her parents were down for the night, she packed the wagon with her belongings and her customers' linens.

Following a fitful night's lack of sleep, she slipped out of her parents' home and headed toward the Seaside Inn. During the night, she had decided to ask Richard Arman if she could rent a room, at least for a couple of days, until she could find a small place she could afford, or find someone to rent a place with. Or she would travel north and visit with Mercy. In either event, she would need a place to stay until she knew where she would make her home.

She pulled into the backyard of the Seaside Inn and climbed down off the wagon. She would need to return it to her father later in the day. She had her basins, washboards and the other tools of her trade packed, as well. The backyard of the inn was large enough to set them in the corner without interfering with the customers and the garden.

"Good morning, Mrs. Martin." Manny beamed. "What's all this?"

"I am moving. Has Mr. Arman surfaced this morning?"

"Not that I could tell." Manny made a beeline for the outhouse.

Grace grabbed the fresh linens for the inn and headed toward the back door.

Richard Arman came out, eyebrows raised. "What's all this?"

# Chapter 5

Richard couldn't believe his eyes. Mrs. Martin's wagon was loaded for...for what? Then he noticed the large basins and pots. "Are you moving?"

"Yes." She hustled past him and went into the kitchen.

Richard followed. "Will you still be working for me?"

"For the time being, if you continue to want my services. Actually, I was hoping to rent a room."

"With all that?" He pointed to the very full wagon.

"That's not all of my belongings. But yes, I'm hoping to find a suitable place that I can afford. In the meantime, I'd like to rent a room from you. I will need to store my belongings, however. My father will want his horse and wagon returned."

"Uh, sure. You can rent a room. It's a dollar a day..." He let his words trail off. He didn't rent rooms to women. But he couldn't let Mrs. Martin not have a roof over her head. And it was practical for her to live here to prepare the early-morning breakfast. "We'll discuss this after the morning meal. If you don't mind."

"Not at all."

Richard knew he was more startled than objecting to her staying at the inn but... "Forgive my confusion, Mrs. Martin. There will be eleven for breakfast this morning."

"Very well. I have a Spanish potato casserole ready to heat and serve. I thought we could have ham steaks and eggs this morning."

"Sounds wonderful. I'll be looking forward to it." Richard stepped toward the hallway leading to his room, hoping he sounded more nonchalant then he felt. "Excuse me. I'll dress for breakfast."

He heard Mrs. Martin pour out some water and wash her hands. He couldn't imagine the argument that must have ensued at her parents' house to make her pack all her belongings and leave. No doubt about it, she was in trouble. And worst of all, his harsh edge wouldn't have made her comfortable. He needed to hire someone, too, but his finances were such that he wouldn't be able to afford to for several weeks.

Richard removed his housecoat and finished dressing for the day. He selected his gray pinstriped pants with a white shirt and a burgundy vest. He finished it off with a burgundy bow tie and his black coat without tails. The bottom of the jacket extended to halfway down his thighs. In another week or two, he probably would have to wear his summer clothing, but the air was cool this morning. Richard glanced in the mirror and made the proper adjustments, finishing off with a final comb through his hair. He always concerned himself with his appearance, especially when he had female guests.

And that was what concerned him. He rented to seamen, not women, Mrs. Robbins being the exception. If he rented a room to Mrs. Martin, how long would she stay? Would he need to be careful for her welfare? Generally speaking, he didn't run into trouble with his tenants because they were always male, or attached to a husband. In this case, she would be alone, sharing a single bathing room with several men. Richard shook off the horrific image. He could not put her in harm's way. Nor could he risk having his tenants concerned about the amount of time a lady would spend in a bathing room. On the other hand, most men used the washbasins in their rooms.

"Jesus, grant me wisdom here." Perhaps it would be workable for a couple of days. He could even help her find a small cottage to rent.

"Yes!" With renewed determination, he decided to help Mrs. Martin find her new home. He headed down toward the dining area where the sweet smells of a hearty breakfast awaited. The table was full, not only with food but with eager customers, as well. Manny sat at the head of the table, taking Richard's usual chair. He glanced over. "Sorry, Richard. I'm almost done."

Everyone was having breakfast this morning. There were men standing against the wall, balancing their plates in one hand and feeding themselves with a fork in the other. "Sit, Manny. I'll go see if Mrs. Martin needs a hand."

Richard escaped into the kitchen. "Can I help?"

She shook her head. "I thought you said it was going to be eleven?"

"That was the number that signed up last night. I think your cooking is bringing them in from the streets."

Grace Martin let out a nervous chuckle. "Perhaps. But we'll run out of food before we run out of mouths to feed."

"Tell me what you need and I'll…"

She glanced at him, and her mouth dropped open.

"What?" He mentally scanned his image in the mirror. Nothing was out of place, at least he hoped not.

"Nothing. It's a handsome outfit you have on today, Mr. Arman." She turned back to the stove and stirred the scrambled eggs.

"Thank you. Now, what can I do to aid you?" He grabbed his apron from the post behind the door, slipped it over his head and tied the ties behind him.

"Those platters can be taken out to the table."

Richard picked up the two platters, one with pancakes, the other with sausage. "Perhaps I should be charging more for breakfast."

Grace Martin's eyes sparkled. She was dressed in ordinary work clothes, but she grabbed his attention. The simple lines of the gray skirt and white blouse highlighted her femininity. He quickly turned his focus back on the food, away from silly notions Manny had put in his head the day before.

As the last of the customers left the dining area, Mrs. Martin brought out some sliced melon as well as orange juice, bacon and sausages. Richard scanned the table in hopes of some of that potato casserole.

"What are you looking for?" she asked as she sat down beside him at the table.

"The Spanish potato casserole."

"That was gone before the first hour was up. I'll put

some aside for you next time. I don't know if you should charge more for breakfast, but you might want to consider charging for second and third helpings. I swear some of those sailors have hollow legs. You'd think they hadn't eaten in months." Grace bowed her head for a moment then picked up her fork.

"You might be onto something there. And yes, sailors do eat their fair share of fresh food when in port. Which brings me to a delicate matter."

She put her fork down and wiped her mouth with a linen napkin.

"I rent rooms to sailors, Mrs. Martin. I don't know if this is the best place for a woman, such as yourself, to stay. I'm happy to have you stay for a few days, and I'll gladly help you find your own cottage to rent. But I don't believe it would be wise to put you at risk. Not all of these men are…I mean… There's only one room per floor for bathing and…" Richard felt like a fool fumbling over his words. "I'm sorry, this is not coming out…"

Mrs. Martin patted his hand. "I understand. And you're right, these aren't the best accommodations for a single woman. But if I could stay for a couple of days, maybe a week, just enough time to get myself situated, I'd be extremely grateful."

"Of course a week is agreeable. And I shall not charge you. You're earning more than your keep by helping me. Would you consider working for me every day?"

"I'll consider it."

"I believe there is enough room in the backyard to set up your laundry. Grandmother did all of hers there until failing health made it impossible."

"Mr. Arman, I appreciate you helping me in this way.

I am beside myself in regard to my father. He…" Mrs. Martin paused. "Forgive me, that is a private affair."

Richard smiled. "I believe we can work out an agreeable salary for you. Although I am quite limited in funds at the moment."

"I understand. I'll take whatever hours I can get."

Richard nodded and looked down at his plate. Offering her a full-time position was a foolish thought. He didn't have the resources at the moment. He was out two hundred dollars, and after this morning's breakfast, his food bill was bound to go up.

Grace finished her breakfast, went straight to work cleaning up the kitchen and then onto stripping the beds. She went outside to grab her wagon and discovered it was empty except for the bundle of Mr. Learner's linens. She stood there, dumbfounded. Manny came running out to greet her. "I put your belongings in Richard's shop. Richard and I will return your father's wagon for you."

"Thank you." She would deliver the linens while they returned the wagon. Grace gave Manny the directions for her family home then grabbed the Learners laundry and walked to The Conch. She walked up the back steps and knocked.

Mr. Learner shuffled to the back door. Seeing her, he smiled. "Good morning, Mrs. Martin. How are you today?"

"Exhausted, but well. Here are your clean linens."

He took the proffered bag. "I'm afraid I don't have any for you today. Mrs. Learner is not doing well. I've decided to not rent out any rooms for a while to give her a chance to rest. Could you come once a week for our personal laundry? I hope this won't put you in a bind."

"No, sir. I'll be fine." Then again, how would she be able to afford rent unless the salary from the Seaside Inn was high enough. *Lord, make it so.*

"I'm renting a room at the Seaside Inn for the week. If your situation changes, just send a message."

Mr. Learner gave a halfhearted smile. "I shall, thank you. I'm sorry you and your father couldn't see eye to eye on the matter."

Grace shrugged. What could she say?

Mr. Learner lifted his thin, weathered hand and tapped her on the shoulder. "The Lord will bring you through this storm. I've been following Him for seventy years now, and He's always seen me through. Though there was a time or two when I thought He left me high and dry on a sandbar. But He didn't. He was there. I just didn't see Him right away. Trust in the Lord with all thine heart; and lean not unto thine own understanding."

"Thank you. It's a good Scripture passage to live by."

"It helps."

Grace heard some gentle moans coming from deeper within the house. "Forgive me, I must see to the missus."

"I'll continue to pray for her."

"Thank you. God will get us through this, even if it is time for us to separate." Mr. Learner's eyes watered. "But you know all about that loss, don't you?" He gave her a hug and shuffled off toward his wife.

Grace turned and left. The Learners were a delightful couple, so much in love. They had seen so many good days together. Her thoughts turned to her own loss. It was hard to lose Micah so early in their marriage. She couldn't imagine what it would be like to lose one's spouse after fifty years. "Father, give them peace."

She walked through the narrow streets toward the Seaside Inn. She had so much to do, setting up her equipment, hanging clotheslines and doing the inn's laundry. With any luck, she wouldn't have to build the posts to hang the clotheslines. Richard had said his grandmother used to do the inn's laundry, so she just had to find out where they were and if they were still solid.

Three hours later the laundry was hung, the pot and washboards rinsed and waiting for the next day's use. Her work done, Grace didn't know where to go. Mr. Arman had not assigned a room to her. Her personal belongings were in his shop, which she didn't feel free to enter. She only felt free to go into the kitchen.

She looked through the ingredients in the pantry and worked on a breakfast menu for the next few days. She could bake some breads, but the temperatures in Florida were rising. Baking in the indoor stove during the heat of the afternoon didn't seem a wise decision. Then of course, there were always good old-fashioned Southern biscuits. They didn't take long to cook and would fill the tummy well enough. She could also make white sausage gravy, a recipe learned from her mother, to pour over the biscuits in the morning.

Grace slipped on her apron and began making up the batter without the liquid contents for easier morning service. She wrote a list of the items needed for the kitchen pantry. No doubt Jorge had used up most, if not all, of Richard Arman's resources. The pantry held an array of hanging meats, sausages and canned goods. Oddly enough, Jorge hadn't depleted the shelves.

"Who's there?" Richard Arman thundered.

Grace let out a startled yelp and immediately covered her mouth. "Forgive me, Mr. Arman." She took a tentative step out of the pantry. "I was taking an inventory to get a better feel for what might be needed for breakfast preparations."

"I'm so sorry, Mrs. Martin. After Jorge..." he stammered. "Forgive me. My tone was completely unacceptable."

"I quite understand," she whispered, clenching her trembling hands.

"Manny and I delivered the wagon to your father. I fear no words were exchanged. Your mother was in tears, and your father simply nodded."

Grace sucked in a quivering breath. "Thank you. You've been most kind. May I ask which room I shall be renting? And do I have permission to enter your barn to retrieve my belongings?"

Richard Arman coughed and cleared his throat. "I'll set you up in room one. It doesn't have a view, but it is closer to the kitchen."

"Thank you." She reached into the waistband pocket of her skirt, a pocket her good friend Mercy had advised her to sew in. She pulled out five dollars. "I have more in the bank but..."

"Nonsense. I owe you a couple of days' pay. Let's call us even for the week, and please continue your shopping list for the kitchen and pantry." He turned and saw the cloth-covered bowl on the counter. "What is this?"

"The dry ingredients for biscuits in the morning. I'll make a sausage gravy to go over them. Also, I'm wondering if you'd like me to add grits to the morning menu."

"Grits are fine. Most of the boarders tend to be from the North and don't seem to have a hankering for Southern fare. Make a small portion and see how it is received. I'll be happy to have some grits. Cheese grits, perhaps." Richard Arman winked.

Grace chuckled. "Cheese grits it is, Mr. Arman. Here's the list I've completed so far. Would it be acceptable for me to use the kitchen while I'm staying here? I'd like to cook my own meals rather than spend money in a restaurant."

"That would be acceptable, Mrs. Martin. I was planning on making a steak for my dinner. Would you care to join forces? I'll cook the steak, and you can cook the fixings." Richard smiled.

It was perhaps the first genuine smile she had ever seen the man give. Richard Arman wasn't an unpleasant sort, and he certainly wasn't unpleasant to the eye, but he had always maintained a businesslike appearance. "That is most kind. I'll be happy to make some smashed garlic potatoes, and there are many fresh squashes available right now."

"Wonderful. Shall we plan dinner for six?"

"Six is acceptable, thank you. And thank you again for allowing me to stay here. Tomorrow I'll begin my search for permanent housing."

Richard's smile faded. He nodded. "Excuse me. I have some work to attend to." He slipped out the door to the dining area and then limped on to the front parlor and behind the reservation counter.

Grace went back into the pantry and continued to write her list.

"Mrs. Martin," Richard Arman called out. "There is a courier here to see you."

"What?" Grace walked to the front room. A young man, perhaps fifteen years of age, stood there with a folded and wax-sealed paper.

He extended it to her. "You are Mrs. Micah Martin?"

"Yes."

"Have a good day."

Grace looked over the folded paper and examined the seal. A large "S" appeared in the center, taking up the circle from top to bottom and a smaller "W" and "A" appeared in the center horizontally. She broke the seal, read the note and dropped it.

# Chapter 6

Richard came up beside her. The message had clearly stunned her. He wanted to reach out to comfort her, but thought better of it. He picked up the note and folded it. As curious as he might be to read it…it was personal. He ushered her to a chair and sat her down. "Can I get you a glass of water?"

Grace shook her head.

"Are you all right?"

She glanced up and met his gaze. Her brown eyes glistened with unshed tears. Now he really wanted to read the note, but restrained himself. He felt totally helpless. And he was so uncertain how to respond to a lady. He left her for a moment and ran to the Robbins' room.

He knocked on the door. "Mrs. Robbins, can you help me?"

Elaine Robbins opened the door. "What can I do for you, Mr. Arman?"

"I fear Mrs. Martin has had some troubling news, and I believe she is in need of some assistance, or at the very least an empathetic ear. Would you be so kind?"

"Certainly." She turned back to her children, who sat on the floor reading. "I'll be back shortly. Finish your stories then you can go out and play."

"Yes, Momma," the children said in unison.

Richard stepped back and let her precede him down the hallway. "She's going to be staying in room one." Richard pointed to the room at the bottom of the stairs.

"Thank you, Mr. Arman. I'll take it from here."

"Thank you." Richard went to his room and paced. This was another reason not to have a female staying in the inn. He didn't know how to fix a woman's problems, and being a man he liked to be able to fix things. Even if it meant having someone else do the fixing. Richard paused for a moment. Which is exactly what he'd done. He had found the right person to help. He took in a deep breath and threw his shoulders back. Perhaps having a woman about wasn't such a bad idea after all.

He exited his room as Mrs. Martin and Mrs. Robbins entered room one. In the kitchen he found Manny entering with a couple of bags in tow. "Where's Mrs. Martin's room? I thought I'd bring her belongings in."

Richard glanced down at the long list on the counter that Grace Martin had been compiling. "You'd better leave them outside her door, room one. She's had a bit of bad news I'm afraid, and she's in there with Mrs. Robbins."

"Oh. How much more can go wrong for that poor woman?"

"I don't know."

"I'll leave them outside her door. Then I've got some shrimp calling my name tonight."

"Fishing?"

"You betcha. Nothing like a free meal from the sea. You want some?"

"Sure, if you wouldn't mind catching enough for Mrs. Martin, as well. I can't imagine she has enough funds to pay for her housing and food."

"Well, you could fix that, ya know." Manny winked.

Richard wagged his head. "Don't even start."

"I'm just sayin'."

"Well, don't." He already had way too many thoughts in that direction. And while he'd like to help Mrs. Martin, he didn't see how offering marriage to a man like himself would be beneficial to her at all.

"All right. I'll try and get some oysters, too."

"Not too many. I'm not certain what we have for canning materials. Mrs. Martin has been making a list of what we need for the pantry."

"She's really something. Let me take care of her bags, then I'll get my shrimping nets from the back of the barn."

Manny's fishing and shrimping did help the fact that he only paid ten dollars a month. Manny was an exception. He had access to the kitchen but seldom used it. Richard would make a seafood dish for the two of them when Manny went fishing in much the same way his grandmother had treated Manny for the past decade. Perhaps, Richard thought, he could convince him to go deer hunting, or better yet, wild pig hunting. The way they'd been going through sausage and bacon, it would help with the budget.

Richard headed out to the barn and began working on

his sailboat. He raised his hand and traveled down the hull where he'd been sanding the last time. It was almost as smooth as a baby's bottom. "Why'd I think of that?" Richard groaned. "Manny."

Richard spent the next couple of hours working in the barn. The pink glow of the sun setting in the west painted the evening sky by the time he wiped his hands and closed up the barn. Outside he saw the empty clotheslines. Mrs. Martin must have come out and removed the laundry. Inside the kitchen he could smell the scrumptious aromas of prepared food. He patted his noisy stomach. "I'll put the steak on in a minute," he called out to no one in particular, but knew Grace Martin had to be in earshot.

A stampede of footfalls on the stairs drew his attention to the front desk where he found one of his customers waiting. "Are you selling dinners now?" the eager sailor asked.

"No, sir. Sorry. We have several fine restaurants in town," Richard answered.

The young sailor—what was his name? Oh yeah, Gary Sandwich—slumped his shoulders. "The wonderful smells from the kitchen have had my stomach gurgling all afternoon. Reminds me of my mother's cooking. What's the occasion?"

"I'm certain Mrs. Martin was preparing food for tomorrow's breakfast."

"You said it was a dollar, right?"

"Yes." Richard was certain the cost of breakfast would be going up.

The young sailor took out two silver dollars from his pocket. "I'll take two. If you have a way of allowing me to take one with me."

Richard chuckled, and both men turned as Grace came to the doorway of the dining area. Giving a nod and a polite smile, she said, "We'll find something for you to pack a second meal in for you, Mr. Sandwich. However, if Mr. Arman is agreeable, there will be some additional pastries for sale, as well. Separate from the breakfast meal."

"Are those what I smelled cooking this afternoon?"

"No, that was a special dessert for Mr. Arman."

Richard raised his eyebrows and narrowed a questioning gaze on Mrs. Martin. She glanced down at the floor then met his gaze and mouthed the words "Thank you." He could feel the smile rise before he could stop it.

"Can I pay you to make me whatever you made for him?"

Grace chuckled. "That, too, is up to Mr. Arman. This is his establishment."

Gary Sandwich's eyes implored Richard's. Richard cleared his throat. "Not at this time, Mr. Sandwich. I will need to speak with Mrs. Martin about costs and whether or not…"

He turned and looked at Mrs. Martin. "Is there enough to share?"

Her chuckle turned to a ripple of laughter. "Yes. But not enough for all the residents."

"If you'll not speak a word of this, you may have some, after we've finished our meal."

"Thank you, thank you. I'm going to town for dinner. What was it you were cooking?"

"Coconut surprise. It's a dish my husband, Micah, loved."

"Your husband is a lucky man." Gary Sandwich headed

toward the door. "Oh, by the way, Manny said to let you know he'll be coming in late from shrimping."

"Thank you, Mr. Sandwich." Richard turned to Grace. "Does that happen often?"

"People referencing my late husband as if he were still alive?"

Richard nodded.

"Often enough. I imagine it will happen a lot more while I'm working for you. Speaking of which, I have the sides ready for our dinner. I'm looking forward to our steak."

Richard glanced down at his sawdust-covered overalls. "I'll clean up and get them cooking shortly."

"Thank you, Mr. Arman. Thank you for all that you've been doing for me. I appreciate it so much."

"It is my pleasure, Mrs. Martin. Excuse me."

Grace watched as Mr. Arman went into his room. It stood apart from the rest of the inn. She imagined it had given his grandparents the privacy they needed to keep their personal lives separate from their responsibilities to the inn. Grace couldn't imagine always having people in your home, never having any private time. And yet people like the Learners and the Armans seemed to make it work.

Grace went back to the dining area and finished setting the table. She found some table linens, candlesticks and the fine china that must have been Mr. Arman's grandmother's private set. She was careful not to set the table in a "romantic" fashion, for that was not the relationship she had with Richard Arman. Nor was she looking for that kind of relationship. Instead she hoped she had achieved a moderately formal table.

The note she'd received earlier in the day shocked and surprised her. How could someone from Micah's past set a claim against her? Micah didn't own anything of value, and yet William Albert Sears was demanding restitution from Micah's estate. In truth, it was an informal request, but the fact was he'd been tracking down Micah for years. Mrs. Robbins encouraged her to believe that all she had to do was prove that she didn't have possession of the articles in question or the finances to cover their value, and she should be free from this obligation. Mr. Sears, however, had threatened legal action.

Grace glanced back at the table. She would not worry about a frivolous claim. It did not seem important in the grand scheme of things. Her parents, her lack of laundry contracts, the lack of a home, were far more pressing at this time. It was also obvious that Mr. Arman was not comfortable with a female boarder. Hopefully, he would be willing to extend the week if she couldn't find a reasonable place to rent, not that she could afford to live at the Seaside Inn for very long.

Richard Arman leaned in from the doorway to the kitchen. "Mrs. Martin, I'll have the steaks ready shortly. How do you like yours?" He had dressed down from his early-morning outfit but up from the work clothes he wore when working in the barn. Tonight he looked relaxed in casual, sailor-style pants and a blue shirt, the shirtsleeves rolled up over his elbows.

"Medium rare, please."

Mr. Arman nodded and slipped into the kitchen. She heard the back door squeak as he opened it. No doubt he would be cooking the steaks over an open fire on the grill, a particular favorite of Grace's, which of course Mr.

Arman would not know. Grace turned back to the table and scanned it one more time.

She changed her place setting location to one chair farther away from Mr. Arman's. *No sense giving him the wrong impression,* she reasoned.

Back in the kitchen she finished mashing the garlic smashed potatoes then put the final touches on the mild yellow squash. She loved the fresh vegetable and couldn't get enough of it when it was in season. Placing the items in serving dishes, she brought them to the table. The back door squeaked again.

"It smells wonderful in here," Richard Arman said, carrying in a platter with a one-inch-thick steak on it.

"Oh my, that's a good-sized one."

Richard beamed. "Normally I eat about half and save the other half for steak and eggs in the morning. Tonight we feast." Richard rubbed his hands together and sat down, placing the platter in the space between them. "A very appealing table, Mrs. Martin, thank you."

"You're welcome. I don't have the opportunity to cook too often, but I do enjoy it."

He grabbed the smashed potatoes and heaped a huge spoonful onto his plate then handed her the bowl. He moved on to the squash then the steak. "May I lead us in prayer?"

"Yes, please." Grace clasped her hands together and bowed her head.

"Father, thank You for the bounty before us. You are all knowing and we ask for Your direction for Mrs. Martin. Thank you for the settlements I was able to negotiate with various business owners, and bless Manny with his shrimping tonight. Amen."

"Amen."

Grace lifted her fork and knife and glanced over at Richard Arman. He dove into his food as a man driven with a purpose. "The potatoes and squash are excellent. Thank you."

"You're welcome. If you wish, I could make dinner tomorrow night."

He sat back in his chair and chewed his meat slowly. "I have been giving your situation some thought. While I'd love to hire you on full-time, my funds are limited at the moment. Jorge left me with a huge debt."

"I understand, Mr. Arman. I shall be cooking for myself each evening. To prepare an additional amount for another is not difficult. In fact, it is easier and cheaper."

He wiped his mouth with the linen napkin. "We both need to eat, and I have found myself on more than one occasion eating a ham sandwich late in the evening." He nodded his head up and down a few times then looked up and glanced at her. "All right, that will be a blessing for both of us. Tomorrow you should plan on making something with shrimp. Manny tends to bring in quite a haul. No doubt he'll bring in some oysters, as well. Do you know how to can them?"

"Yes. Would you like me to can them for you?"

Mr. Arman paused. "Yes, if that is not an imposition. Summer is coming when it will be too warm for fresh oysters."

"It's not an imposition. Please understand, I am most grateful for your kindness in extending a room for me. What if we barter my pay for the room for the week. That will save you money, I think."

He leaned in toward his plate, his fork still in his hand. "I would be paying you more than the cost of the room. You would be losing money."

Grace shrugged. "A blessing to us both."

He released a pent-up breath. "All right, even exchange for the cooking, but I will continue to pay for the linen service you provide."

"Thank you, you are most kind."

Mr. Arman mumbled something then clarified his words. "You're welcome."

Richard found himself more and more comfortable with a woman underfoot. And his toe, while it still hurt, was finally on the mend. Grace Martin was an industrious sort. Every morning she was up at dawn preparing the morning meal, then she'd work on the laundry. While the sheets and towels were drying, she would go in search of a place to live. And each day she'd come back discouraged, unable to find a place she could afford that was large enough for her laundry service.

Rapid footfalls on the stairs drew his attention back to his customers. "Good morning, Mr. Johnson. Did you rest well?"

"Very. I failed to order breakfast, and others said I was a fool not to. If it is not too late, may I purchase breakfast?"

"The cost is a dollar. However, if you go for a second helping it is an additional fifty cents."

Mr. Johnson pulled a leather billfold from his rear pocket and plopped two dollars on the counter. "I'll probably have thirds. It smells great."

Richard chuckled. "It is. Mrs. Martin has outdone herself this morning." *The way to a man's heart...* Richard stopped his mind from going down that path again. Not only was he comfortable with her at the inn, he was beginning to ask her opinions on various matters where it concerned his customers.

Mr. Johnson followed his nose to the dining room. Richard recorded the income and placed the bills in the lockbox, or "bank" as some referred to it. The bank was a sturdy lockbox of cast iron and sat on the floor. It wasn't that large, but its extra weight did deter opportunistic thieves from running off with it.

"Morning, Mr. Arman," Billy said, as he came out from the dining room rubbing his belly. "Mrs. Martin sure can cook. That shrimp omelet with fresh salsa was excellent. I never knew you could put shrimp in an omelet."

Richard smiled. Grace Martin had been canning shrimp and making shrimp dishes all week. Richard loved shrimp, but after a week he was ready for something else. He looked forward to the roast pork he'd been smoking since yesterday. Tonight he'd finish it off with some of his homemade sauce. His stomach gurgled in anticipation. The one negative about having Mrs. Martin in his kitchen was that he didn't get to do as much cooking as he liked. He enjoyed playing with flavors, and cooking was something he and his grandparents had in common. His father could navigate his way around a stove, grill and smokehouse well enough, but he'd been happy to find a wife who loved doing all the cooking.

Billy was nearly out the front door before Richard answered him. "She is a fine cook."

"Yes, sir." Billy placed his cap on his head. "I'll see you next time I'm in port. A man can't pass up a good meal like that."

Richard's mind flashed to the fact that tomorrow would be Grace's last day staying at the inn, and she still had not found a place to live. Should he reconsider and have her stay for another week?

The bell above the door jangled. Richard looked up and saw a man dressed in an expensive suit. "May I help you?"

"Yes, I've been told that a Mrs. Micah Martin works here."

"Yes, sir."

"May I speak with her?" he said as he removed his gloves and hat. He certainly couldn't be from around here, Richard observed. The temperature was too warm for such layers of finery as this man wore.

"Whom may I say is asking for her?"

"William Sears."

"Have a seat, Mr. Sears. I'll let Mrs. Martin know of your presence."

"Thank you." Mr. Sears sat down in one of the over-stuffed chairs facing the harbor view.

Richard headed back to the kitchen where he found Grace hunched over the stove, her face glowing with sweat.

"Mr. Arman, may I help you?"

"There's a Mr. Sears waiting for you in the front parlor."

Grace staggered and caught her footing. "Mr. William A. Sears?"

"He said he was William Sears. Is there a problem? Should I remove him from the establishment?"

Grace sighed. Her shoulders slumped. She wiped her hands and face with the towel. "No, this is my concern. I'll deal with it."

Richard nodded, scanned the stove and put his apron on. Most of the clients had left for the day. He could finish cooking and serving the meal. He stepped into the dining area and removed some of the empty plates. Manny sat by himself sipping his morning tea.

Almost immediately, raised voices emanated from the front parlor. Mr. Sears was not a happy man. Richard debated as to whether or not to step in. He cleared the plates and returned to the kitchen and placed them beside the sink. It was not his place to interfere with regard to Mrs. Martin's personal life.

But then he heard Manny's voice. "You can't speak in that tone to her. She's a lady and due your respect."

"And who are you, her father?"

"No, I don't have the honor. I'm simply a friend. And I will not have you bullying my friend."

William Sears snickered. "As if you could stop me." There was a pause, and Mr. Sears's comments returned to Mrs. Martin. "You shall do as I ask. You must honor your husband's debt."

Hearing that, Richard stepped into the front parlor. Grace cowered in the chair. "Mr. Sears," Richard said, pointing to the door, "I believe you have overstayed your welcome." Manny placed his hands on his hips. A couple of the boarders came down the stairs to check out the commotion.

"Forgive me," William Sears bellowed in return, "but I have been searching for Mrs. Martin for five years. And now I want what was promised to me."

Richard glanced at Grace.

"As I said to you, Mr. Sears, I do not know of any agreement between you and my husband. And I do not believe the law would require me to settle this debt that you claim to have with my husband. Where is your proof?"

William Sears pulled out a folded piece of paper, a bit tattered by the years, and handed it to Grace Martin.

She opened the note and glanced at it. Her hands began to shake. Tears welled in her eyes. "This is Micah's signature," she whispered.

"Then you will do as I ask?"

She shook her head. "No, sir. I cannot. I will not." Grace stood up and addressed Mr. Sears. "I am not responsible for this debt. I will not pay."

"You'll hear from my attorney." William Sears set his hat upon his head and turned. Richard stood with Manny and the two other male boarders forming a gauntlet to the door. Sears tugged at his collar as if to give himself more breathing space.

"Good day, sir." Richard, open palmed, indicated the front door. Sears scanned the four men and didn't say another word. All eyes stayed focused on him until he shut the door behind him. Then in unison all turned their attention to Grace Martin. She crumpled in the chair and held her hands to her face. The clients left first. Manny mumbled something and headed toward the kitchen.

Richard came up and knelt beside her. He placed a compassionate hand upon hers. "I have an attorney you can speak with, but I believe you are correct. You are not under obligation to this man."

Her brown eyes glazed over with tears. "Thank you. Forgive me, I need to freshen up."

Richard nodded. A lump the size of a pecan lodged in his throat. She got up and ushered herself back to her room. Richard stayed beside the empty chair for a moment. *Dear Lord, how can I help this woman?*

# Chapter 7

As Grace prepared the evening meal, she found herself running over William Sears's words again and again. And then she would visualize the note in Micah's own handwriting. She shook off the thoughts. She would not dwell on this for another moment. Micah never owned anything, and if he had, she would have known about it. Then again, the letter stated that Micah owed Mr. Sears the value of six acres of land and used a portion of his property as collateral. Where? When? She couldn't deny that it was his writing. Micah had a unique way of signing his name. The capital M in both Micah and Martin were large, and on the bottom extending line of the M he would write the rest of his name, as if the M underlined each name.

Then another thought occurred to her. She had spent the entire afternoon searching for a new place to live and found nothing she could afford. If she owned Micah's land...she shook off the thought. It couldn't be possible, could it?

She scribbled a note off to Richard Arman. A visit to Micah's parents was in order. Maybe they could shed some light on William Sears's claim.

She rarely saw Micah's parents. To say they had a strained relationship put it mildly. It's as if they blamed her for Micah's death. But Micah died in battle. It wasn't her fault. If anything, she had tried to encourage him to stay home and not go fight in the War of Aggression. But Micah was passionate and determined, having lost his older brother to the war the year before. As soon as he was of age, he'd left and joined the confederate army, waiting only long enough to marry.

Their marriage was a short one, their courtship had been ongoing since she entered ninth grade and he the tenth. Before she and Micah married, his parents seemed to enjoy her company. Afterward...well, she wouldn't go down that path again. Nothing good came from harboring ill will toward another, nothing, including toward Micah's parents. At the very least they had given Micah life, and he had been a tremendous blessing to her for many years.

She draped her apron over the chair in the kitchen, signed the note to Richard and left the inn and started toward the Martins' ranch. With any luck she could get a ride from the ranch back to the city before it was too dark. They weren't bad people. They just didn't fancy her too much.

Suddenly, she remembered the tablecloth in her trunk and ran into the barn to retrieve it. She should have given it back ages ago but no one else had married in the family since Micah passed. His younger brother was of age now, but she honestly didn't know what had been happening with the Martins since Micah passed away. They had shared a few tears together at Micah's memorial service but that was all.

She walked down the lane out toward the edges of the city and started over the bridge toward the Martins' ranch when a carriage came up beside her. "Evening, Mrs. Martin, can I give you a lift?"

Sadie Hall, a former slave from the Hastings ranch, grinned, looking down from her seat. She and her husband continued to stay on and work for Mr. Hastings as sharecroppers. "I would love one, if it is not too much trouble."

"Where are you headed, child?"

"The Martin ranch."

"I'll be happy to take you. These old bones are telling me there is a storm coming, so the sooner you get there, the better."

"Yes'm." Grace didn't question old folks' bones. They seemed to be a good indicator of bad weather to come.

"Whatcha got there?" Sadie nodded toward the tablecloth.

"It's a wedding gift handed down three generations in Micah's family. I wanted to give it back so they could hand it down for Micah's brother Max when he marries."

"Ah, that's mighty nice. How's you doin' missin' your Micah?"

Grace sighed. "All right, I guess. I still have no desire to marry another."

Sadie placed her rough hand on Grace's knee. "When the good Lord sends ye another, you'll know."

"Thanks. Everyone else is trying to marry me off."

Sadie kept laughing. "It's the way of things, child. After all, you are ready to have children."

Grace groaned.

Sadie continued to laugh and drove the wagon along the road up to the Martins' homestead. She pulled the wagon to a halt in front of the house. Grace jumped down and turned. "Thank you, Sadie."

"Do you need a ride home, child? I's got some time."

Grace paused. She could use the ride home but she had no idea how long her conversation with the Martins would take. "Thank you, I'll find a ride."

Sadie nodded and took the reins. With a gentle flick of her wrists, the horse pulled forward.

Grace walked up the stairs and reached to knock on the painted white doors. But they opened before her hand hit the door. "Grace, what can we do for you?" Mrs. Martin smiled.

"I've come about a couple of things. May I come in?"

"Yes, yes, by all means." Mrs. Martin stepped back, opening the door farther. Grace walked into the home she had not been in for five years. She wondered how Micah would have felt about how his parents had treated her after his passing. "Come to the front parlor." She rang a bell and one of their former slaves came out attired in a simple gray dress with a white apron that covered most of her uniform. "Elsa, would you prepare some tea and biscuits for Grace and me?"

"Yes, ma'am." Elsa bowed and hurried to the kitchen.

"Come, Grace. I see you have the wedding tablecloth." She led the way into the parlor and offered Grace a cushioned armchair.

"Yes. I felt since Micah and I didn't have children, I should return it so it could be passed on to Max and his children."

"That's very kind of you, thank you." Mrs. Martin

took the tablecloth and gently caressed it. "What has changed that you have decided to return it? Are you getting married?"

"No, ma'am. I moved out of my father's house and decided it was the right thing to do while I was packing away my belongings."

"Ah."

"Mrs. Martin, I had a visit from a Mr. William A. Sears earlier today. He showed me a note in which Micah promised to give him six acres of his land as collateral if he failed to meet his debt. Did you know Micah owned land?"

Mrs. Martin paled.

Elsa came into the room. "Elsa, run and get Mr. Martin, immediately." Mrs. Martin's complexion changed from pale to red. "So," she huffed, "you want Micah's land. I knew you didn't love him."

"How dare you! I loved Micah with all my heart. I haven't been able to even consider marrying another, and I knew nothing of this land. Are you telling me Micah has property, which by law would be my property?"

Mrs. Martin's nostrils flared. "Get out!"

Grace stood. "Fine, I'll let Mr. Sears's lawyers contact you. I'm done with you and your entire family." She stomped out of the house and slammed the door shut. The sun was setting. She would need to hustle back to get into the city before nightfall.

So, Micah did own land, and she would have had resources to live on if she'd known about it. Now she would need to hire a lawyer.

Richard reread the note left by Grace Martin. There was no indication as to where she'd gone, only that she would not be joining him for dinner this evening. Oddly enough, in a week's time, he'd become very comfortable sharing the dinner hour with her.

Manny walked into the kitchen. "Where are you headed tonight?" Richard asked.

"I'm fixin' to have a night with some of my old shipmates." Manny grinned. "Tonight's the night I get together with my buddies."

"Is it that time of the month again?"

"Yes, sir. Now if you'll excuse me, I'm off."

"Certainly." Richard paused. "Manny, do you know where Mrs. Martin was going this afternoon?"

"No. She did stop in the barn and took a blanket or something out with her. She headed west."

"Thanks."

"What's troubling you?"

"Well, that visit from Mr. Sears this morning, for one. For another, the note she left wasn't all that revealing. Not that she's obligated to tell me her whereabouts but…" He paused. "I don't have a good feeling about it. The sun is setting and soon it will be dark. What do you think?"

"I think if Mr. Sears is claiming her husband has property that belongs to him, she would go to his parents and try to clear up the matter."

Richard nodded and nibbled the inside of his cheek. "You're probably right. I'll get the buggy ready and see if I can locate her before it gets too dark."

"I'll give you a hand. We need to protect that woman."

Richard couldn't agree more. Grace Martin's care and protection seemed to fall under his responsibilities. He probably didn't have any right to feel that way, but she was an employee and also a client. He'd do the same for anyone else in the same situation, wouldn't he? But he had to admit to himself that he felt a growing attraction to the blond, brown-eyed beauty. He prayed she wasn't aware of his feelings. Nothing good would come out of his admitting his attraction.

He fetched his hat and procured his buggy from the barn then grabbed the harness and equipment to hook up his Belgian Draft horse, Brownie.

Once fastened, Manny and Richard climbed aboard. Richard glanced over to his right. "You do realize there isn't room for Mrs. Martin if we find her?"

Manny looked at the limited seating. "Ah, drop me off at the edge of town, and I'll make my way to my friends. In the meantime, I'm another set of eyes."

"That is acceptable. Thank you."

"Nothing to thank me for yet. Mrs. Martin is a fine woman. It's sad to see so much tragedy in such a young life. Are you aware that her father is pressuring her to remarry?"

"Yes."

"Well, it ain't right, I tell ya. No man should have the right to tell his grown child, a widow mind you, who she is to marry or when she is to marry. It just ain't right."

"I agree." They made their way through the narrow streets of the old town and headed to the outskirts of the city. Most of the ranches were outside the city limits.

They approached the bridge that crossed the river and inner harbor. A small figure approached in the darkness. "Grace, is that you?" Richard called out. Her head swung upward and she waved.

Just then the heavens opened up, and it began to rain. Deep, thick Florida raindrops started lightly then came in earnest. Richard maneuvered the buggy closer to Grace Martin. "Come on, Mrs. Martin. We'll make room for you." Manny jumped down and helped her up into the buggy.

"Thank you. How'd you know where to find me?"

"We figured Mr. Sears's visit would prompt you to speak with your in-laws."

Richard slid over as far as he could. Grace climbed in and settled beside him. Manny wedged in beside her. He lifted his arm and wrapped it around the chilled woman's shoulders. "Forgive me for getting so personal, ma'am."

"I understand, Manny, and I am not offended."

The rain beat down harder. "Where would you like me to drop you off, Manny?" Richard had to shout over the sound of the pounding rain.

"Jasper's would be mighty nice. Don't mind me if I don't come back tonight. If'n this rain don't let up, I'll hole up at Jasper's for the night."

"Forgive me for not knowing where Jasper lives but what street is he on?"

Manny gave the directions.

Grace gripped her sides. Richard could see that she'd been crying. He wanted to wrap his arm around her and protect her from anything further. What could have happened? he wondered. She never spoke of her in-laws. Perhaps they weren't very close. Richard turned off King St. and headed north up Cordova toward Cuna.

The driving rain intensified. He turned onto Cuna in the direction Manny had pointed. "That's the house, thank you," Manny shouted over the storm, then turned toward Grace. "Whatever you need me for, I'm here to help ya."

"Thank you, Manny."

Manny nodded and ran toward the front porch of the house, each footfall throwing up geysers of water.

Richard flicked the reins. "Come on, Brownie, let's head home."

Grace shifted a bit toward the right. Richard adjusted himself, as well. "Thank you for coming to my rescue."

"I'm glad we found you at the beginning of the storm."

"Sadie said there was a storm coming."

"Yes, it feels like this one may last quite a few hours." Richard turned the carriage down toward his street. "Grace, we need to talk."

Grace nodded. "I don't know what to say. These are my troubles."

Richard reached over and placed a hand over hers. "Let me be a friend and see if I can help you with all of these claims and such."

Grace trembled under his touch. He removed his hand and drove into his yard. "I'll meet you in the house."

Grace ran into the house. She was damp, cold and shaking.

As much as she would love to have a shoulder to lean on, she wasn't certain Richard Arman was the one. Then again, he had cared enough to drive out into the storm to find her. The same could not be said of her in-laws, who had been cheating her out of Micah's inheritance for the past five years. Nor her parents, who were trying to dictate her life.

But the deepest hurt of all was Micah. Why would Micah have kept the land a secret from her? She thought their relationship had been one of love, openness and trust. They were so young, yet they had stayed together all through their schooling days. How was it that he could have owned land and she not have known about it? And obviously it was more than six acres of land. Then there was the question as to why Micah needed money that required putting up six acres as collateral.

She rubbed the back of her neck. Perhaps she should speak to Richard. She needed someone who was objective to help her gain perspective. But was he objective? He'd been nothing but a gentleman around her, and yet she felt an underlying attraction to him. Not that she would ever act upon it. For she was certain she was not the kind of woman Richard Arman would be attracted to.

Grace went to her room for dry clothing. She chose a plain housedress. She liked dressing down and feeling relaxed, something she'd learned from the Hastings family. Although the family had money, they lived casually.

Richard Arman, she reflected, dressed like the Hastings family. Grace liked that. Perhaps Richard was a good choice, she thought with a smile as she exited her room.

Standing in her doorway with his fist raised to knock was Richard. Their eyes met. Grace swallowed.

"I'm sorry," he apologized. "Shall we go to the den where we'll have some privacy?"

Grace nodded and headed toward the den. Richard stepped aside and allowed her to lead the way. He was a gentleman. He had all the refinement of the perfect host.

She took a seat and he chose one across from her. He waited for her to begin. Grace sighed. "So, what would you like to know?"

"Nothing that you don't want to tell me." Richard shifted. "Mrs. Martin, please understand I do not need to know what's going on but..." He paused for a moment, looked down at his lap then looked back up at her. "I do have an attorney who might be of some service."

"I'm afraid I am in need of legal counsel. It appears that Micah did own property and that my in-laws knew about it." Grace turned and glanced over to the doorway. Seeing no one there, she continued. "I'm having a hard time coming to terms with their deceit." She began to shake. "I have no idea how much land Micah had, or when he purchased or received it. And to know that he may have provided for me in the event that something happened to him…" Grace jumped up and started to pace. "I just can't believe what they've allowed me to go through."

She stopped her pacing. Richard stayed in his seat. She sat back down.

"Mrs. Martin." He paused. "You will need to speak to an attorney. Mr. Sears seems to have a legitimate claim on Micah's estate."

"And that's another thing. Why would Micah borrow the kind of money worth six acres of land? What did he need the cash for? It's almost like Micah had a separate life I knew nothing about."

"Perhaps. But don't be too quick to judge your husband's intentions. Rest in what you knew about him. You said you grew up together. Can he be that different from the man you married?"

Grace shook her head. "I don't know. I honestly don't know anymore. It's all so confusing."

He changed the subject. "I'd like you to know, if you're willing…I would like for you to stay on for another week."

"Really?" Grace couldn't believe her ears. "Oh, goodness, thank you, thank you so much! I haven't been able to find a place I can afford. And just thinking about legal expenses…" She let her words trail off.

"Nonsense. It's practical. You've been a tremendous help. I appreciate your service."

"Thank you, Mr. Arman. You've been so helpful to me, too."

Richard smiled for a fraction of a second. "You're welcome. I'll write a letter of introduction to my attorney and give you the address in the morning. Try to have a good night's sleep. I know these things can be upsetting. But I believe the Good Lord doesn't give us more than we can handle."

Grace snickered. "I believe it, too. I just wish God didn't think I could handle so much."

Richard chuckled. "Well, let's call it a night. Morning comes early when we have to prepare breakfast for our guests."

"That it does. Thank you again." Grace stood and, with a subtle nod of her head, walked past him to her room, the events of the day replaying again and again in her mind. She felt adrift from the confusion, the hurt, the betrayal, all swirling around in her mind. She could not come to any conclusions apart from the need to secure an attorney. She didn't want to be mad at her in-laws, but she couldn't help it. They had robbed her of her inheritance from Micah. The only place she had to run for safety was back home with parents who treated her as a child. And then there was the generosity of Richard Arman, his kindness, his concern…he'd even rescued her. The Seaside Inn felt more like home than any other place she'd been in since Micah's death.

Grace fell to her knees and cried out to her heavenly Father, pouring out all the thoughts that were swimming in her head. "Please Lord," she pleaded, "help me not be angry. I can feel myself getting bitter if I stay on this path of anger. I don't want that."

The patter of the heavy raindrops slapped against

her window. She glanced up as the sky illuminated with streaks of lightning. She counted one, one thousand, two, one thousand. "Bam!" The rumble of thunder shook the house. The actual strike was two miles away, she estimated, but it was powerful enough. The menacing sky seemed to merge with her heart, all dark and rumbling. Another streak of lightning flashed, revealing some of the white clouds within the gray. God was still with her within the disturbance. And He was still in control, even though everything looked chaotic at the moment.

## Chapter 8

Richard penned a letter of introduction to his attorney, Ben Greeley. He blew the ink dry then folded the paper in thirds. He took out his sealing wax, lit the wick and let the wax drip on the paper. He pressed the brass signet into the soft wax and held it there for a moment.

He wanted to escort Grace to Ben's office but thought it better not to. He'd already begun to hear murmurs about his renting a room to his laundress and cook. For the most part, folks seemed to think it was practical. A few, thankfully not as common, thought it inappropriate. He couldn't stop gossip, and he couldn't change the hearts of those who always thought the worst of people. However, he could affect how he and Grace were perceived in the community. Grace Martin did not need any further trouble, and gossip would only cause her further grief.

He exited his room and went to the kitchen where he

saw Grace outside working on the laundry. "Mrs. Martin," he called out to her.

Her head bobbed up. She was stirring the laundry in the large pot. He'd seen ringer washing machines being advertised and wondered if they might provide a better alternative. Perhaps he should ask one of the larger hotels in the area. "Just a minute," she replied.

Richard stepped back into the kitchen. The room was spotless. No one would have known that she had produced a breakfast feast for twenty people earlier this morning. Manny stepped into the room. "Whacha up to today?"

"Nothing much, working on my boat."

Manny grunted. "I'm not going shrimping today. I've had enough."

Richard chuckled. "You and me both."

"Some of the guys were talking about going pig hunting. Are you up for smoking?"

"If you catch one, I'll be happy to smoke it."

"Good, 'cause I'm looking forward to seeing what Mrs. Martin can do with some pork."

Richard's stomach rumbled. "I wouldn't mind some of that myself."

"She said you are going to let her stay at the inn for another week. Glad to see you relying on some of that good sense the Lord gave ya." Manny leaned closer. "Did ya find out what her in-laws did or said that upset her so?"

"Not my place to say, but I am having her speak with my attorney."

Manny leaned back on his heels. "Good, good. Someone needs to protect that woman."

Grace's footfalls tapped out her arrival on the wooden stairs. "What do you need, Mr. Arman?"

Richard held out the letter. "This is a letter of introduction for you to give to my attorney, Benjamin Greeley. His address is on the front."

She wiped her hands on her apron then reached for the proffered letter. "Thank you."

Richard nodded. "Excuse me. I have some other business to attend to." No sense lingering. He wouldn't want Manny encouraging gossip around town. He headed down the hall to room five. He hadn't seen the middle-aged sailor leave this morning or come to breakfast. It was time to check and see if he left or was feeling poorly. Richard knocked. No answer. He knocked again. Again there was no answer. Slowly, he opened the door. John Silva lay on the bed. Too still. Richard stepped into the room and approached the bed. He checked for a pulse. Mr. Silva's body was cold.

Richard closed the room, put a do-not-disturb sign up and sent a message to the sheriff, then went to look for Manny. He didn't believe any crime had been committed but he wasn't about to disturb the room. That wasn't his job. He had learned that the first time a customer expired on the premises. His grandmother had warned him it could happen. It wasn't a common occurrence, but did happen a handful of times over the years his grandparents were in charge of the inn.

Unfortunately, this was the second time since Richard had taken over the Seaside Inn. Fortunately, he knew what to do. First, get the sheriff. Second, gather the information about Mr. Silva and have it ready for the sheriff. Third, call the mortician. Fourth, clean the room and clean the mattress well. And finally, go through Mr. Silva's personal effects in order to find his relations.

"Manny?" Richard tapped on Manny's door. Hearing

no response, he knew he'd left for his hunting expedition. Richard had hoped Manny would be able to lend him a hand removing and returning the mattress. For tonight the room was unrentable.

"Mr. Arman?" Richard turned at the sound of Grace's voice. Time seemed to slow as she approached in a soft, flowing motion. A few wisps of stray blond hair brushed across her right eye, caressing her face.

"Yes?" he stammered.

She glanced at him then around the hallway. "Is something the matter?"

Richard didn't want to hide it from Grace, but he certainly didn't want to upset her. She'd had enough upsets in the past week. "Mr. Silva died in his sleep last night," he answered before she asked.

"Oh." She paused. "Oh, goodness…. What happened?"

"I don't know. That is something for the sheriff and doctor to figure out."

She nodded. "Of course. Um," she stammered, "I was going to head to Mr. Greeley's office, unless you need me to stay or anything."

Richard smiled. "There is nothing you can do. Thank you for asking. Go, settle your affairs. Would you like me to mention it to the sheriff?"

She hesitated. "I suppose I should. I'm going to the town clerk's office, as well, to check on what kind of land deeds Micah might have registered. I'll probably do that before I see Mr. Greeley. Oh, I don't know…"

Richard reached out and placed a hand upon her shoulder. "It will be all right. Trust the Lord, Grace," he said, whispering her name.

She gazed up into his eyes. The brown of her eyes

sparkled with shafts of black that reached the outer edges and encircled them, enhancing their rich, full color. Richard swallowed.

"Thank you," she whispered.

Grace paused for a moment then turned to leave. He wished there was more he could do but knew he couldn't. "God's blessings on your day, Mrs. Martin."

She turned. "And on yours, as well, Mr. Arman."

Sheriff Bower sauntered in through the front door as Grace was leaving. He held the door open for her and she paused. "Sheriff, Mr. Arman will fill you in on a little drama I've been having recently and thought you should probably know about it."

"Are you safe?"

"Yes. My life is not in danger, just my future." She slipped out the door.

The sheriff turned toward Richard. "Is she being melodramatic?"

Grace spent an hour in the town clerk's office searching the land records. It was disturbing to see Micah's name, a hundred and twenty acres and "classified entry" as cash, paid in full. *How could he have done that without my knowing?* she wondered.

The clerk made a legal copy of the town records of the land purchase, including its location, and handed her the certified paper. Now she began to wonder if Micah had left her a will. His parents said there wasn't one, and she'd known nothing of him writing one. Although he had told her he'd taken care of her before he left. And she was able to stay in the small cottage they were renting at the time of their marriage for the entire time he was in the service. It wasn't until a couple of months after the announcement of his death that she'd been forced to move back in with her parents. The money Micah had been providing for the rent stopped coming after his death. The couple who owned the cottage they had rented had no choice but to ask her to leave.

She walked up the brick stairs of Greeley's office. The white trimmed door and black wrought-iron railings all gave the appearance of business without affluence. She decided she might just like this Mr. Greeley. Of course, he had Richard's approval, as well. She opened the door and stepped into a small, sparsely furnished waiting room. A woman with her gray hair pulled back into an elegant chignon sat at an organized oak desk. "May I help you?" she asked.

"Yes, please. Mr. Richard Arman from the Seaside Inn recommended that I speak with Mr. Greeley about some personal legal matters. Is he in?"

The woman smiled. "Yes, just a moment and I'll see if he's free to speak with you. What is your name, miss?"

"Mrs. Grace Martin, thank you." Grace handed her the letter of introduction from Richard.

The woman got up, tapped on the door to a back office and walked in. She came out a moment later. "He said you could come in, in just a few minutes. He's working on a case and will need to put some papers away. Please have a seat."

Grace sat down in one of the upholstered chairs. She fingered the paperwork she received from the town clerk's office. The attorney's door opened. A thin man with broad shoulders, perhaps thirty years of age, stepped out of the office. "How may I help you, Mrs. Martin?" He held the door and extended his hand for her to walk through.

Grace found her footing and marched into Mr. Greeley's office. A mahogany desk, bookcases and filing cabinets lined the room. In front of his desk were two captain's chairs, and she sat in one. "It concerns the death of my husband. A man claiming to be owed six acres of his land for a debt he didn't pay..." She handed him a paper. "It appears my in-laws knew about this land and have kept it from me."

He scanned the legal draft the town clerk had produced for her then glanced up. "Perhaps you should start from the beginning."

And she did. She told him about her childhood romance, their wedding, his death, the lack of concern his parents had for her after Micah passed and then the events of the past week.

He sat back in his chair. "It appears to me that your husband must have put together a will. I know the military recommends that for each of its soldiers. I'll need to do some research. I'll find out how and when he purchased the land, if he had a will and, if so, if you are the beneficiary. If you are, then we shall begin legal action against your in-laws, who have been claiming the land as their own. You should be aware this will probably involve a court hearing. I'll try to settle the matter out of court but, with Mr. Sears involved, I can't imagine it not going to court."

Grace nibbled her lower lip. "I see no other alternative, as well."

Mr. Greeley nodded, stood up and extended his hand. "Then I shall get right on it."

"But there is one more thing. I don't have the funds to pay you."

"Actually you do, if you own a hundred and twenty acres of land. We can hold a portion of that as collateral and stipulate that in our contract. My fees are modest, and I'm happy to help. Plus you've been highly recommended by Mr. Arman. I shall keep my costs to a minimum. We can work out a payment plan, as well."

"Thank you." Grace got up. "You don't know how much it means to me to know someone is going to be my advocate in court."

"You're welcome. I'll also speak with Mr. Sears and his attorney. Together we'll file the claim against your in-laws."

Grace's back stiffened. She didn't want to be rude and take a hard line about this, but they had cheated her. And cheated her out of a significant amount of money. It wasn't right. "Thank you." She nodded. She couldn't say anything else. The hurt was deeper than she anticipated. The knowledge of what they had been doing to her for the past five years was too much to comprehend.

She returned to the inn and found her mother waiting for her in the lobby. "Grace, it's so good to see you." Her mother embraced her.

Grace hugged her mother with equal enthusiasm. "It's good to see you, too. What brings you to town?"

"You."

Grace led her mother to the sitting area for guests. "What do you mean?" Grace's mind flittered back to the events of the past week with Mr. Sears and her in-laws.

"We've missed you. We want you to come home."

Grace smiled. "No, I won't be coming home, Mother. For the time being this is my home. I'm working to pay for my room and board and I still have my laundry business." Albeit with only one customer.

"But your father has found some potential suitors. In fact, there's a young man who's very interested in meeting you."

Grace closed her eyes. "No, Mother, thank you. I can't entertain the thought of being courted by anyone at this time."

"Why not? Don't you want to get married?"

Richard stepped into the hallway and overheard Grace and her mother talking. He didn't want to interrupt a private conversation, so he placed the soiled mattress down and returned to the room. He opened the window and closed the door.

His compassion for Grace overflowed. She said her parents had been pressuring her—he couldn't believe they were still trying. He walked back to the entrance of the sitting area and paused just inside the hallway toward the rental rooms.

"Mother, please, stop."

"Your father says there's been some talk about improprieties with regard to you and Mr. Arman."

"Mother!" Grace's voice rose to a pitch Richard had not heard before. "How dare you bring me gossip and rumors? You know me, and you know I would never..." Grace let her words trail off.

"Grace, dear. I didn't say I believed the rumors. I just wanted you to know what people are starting to say to your father."

"Well, how dare they? And why would Father not come to my defense and put down any such foolish rumors?" Grace began to pace.

Richard felt horrible hearing this private conversation. On the other hand, he felt it was his duty to clarify the situation and defend Grace. And yet it wouldn't be right for him to intrude. He sat down in the hallway and prayed.

"Mother, please leave. I find that if I were to say something to you right now I would regret it for the rest of my life. Please, go home. I appreciate your concern, but I can take care of myself."

Her mother huffed and got up. Richard stayed put well after he heard the front door close.

"You can come out now, Mr. Arman."

"I'm sorry," he said as he entered the room. "I didn't mean to intrude on your private conversation."

"No, I must apologize. Can you believe? No, never mind. It just adds to the kinds of days I've been having lately. Perhaps it is time for me to move and join my friend in Massachusetts."

Grace sat back down in one of the high-backed over-stuffed chairs. She looked so small and fragile. "What did the lawyer say?"

She closed her eyes. Richard sat down in the chair beside her. He wanted to scoop her up in his arms and tell her not to worry. That he would protect her. But it wasn't his place. Instead he would simply be a friend.

"I stopped by the town clerk's office and discovered that Micah owned a hundred and twenty acres shortly before he left to fight the war. Can you believe that the Martins knew about this and hid it from me?"

"I'm sorry." What else could he say?

Her eyes searched his for a moment. "None of this has been your fault, no matter what rumors might be spreading. Truthfully, I can't help but wonder if my own father is behind the rumors, hoping to force me to do his will. Then again, that would affect his reputation, and he would not want that."

Richard reached over and opened his hand. She responded and placed her hand in his. "Let's pray about this, shall we?

"Father," Richard began, "we can't begin to under-stand why all these events are unfolding in Grace's life but we ask for Your guidance and peace. In Jesus' Name, Amen."

"Amen. And thank you, Richard." She blushed.

He released her hand. They talked for a few minutes more about what the lawyer would be doing over the next few days, then Grace stood up. "Well, I have chores that need to be finished."

"As do I." Richard headed back to the hallway where the mattress stood. He carried it out to the backyard and began scrubbing it down. His grandmother had insisted on cleanliness through and through. She'd taught him a lot about the business, about people and how to respond to them. But she never prepared him for the emotions he was feeling right now.

He wanted to take Grace's parents and force them to somehow see what they were doing wrong with their daughter. And he really wanted to haul the Martins out to the back of the barn and tan their hides. How could they have treated their own son's wife so poorly? But he knew that families weren't always at their best when it came to dealing with their own. Or in this case, trust-ing Grace with Micah's inheritance. He actually pitied them. They had no idea how tenderhearted and brilliant the woman was.

Finished cleaning the mattress, Richard glanced over and saw Grace taking the linens off the clothesline. She truly was a remarkable woman, and so industrious. He certainly saw why Micah had married her.

He moved inside the barn and picked up a sanding block. He just didn't know what else he could do. He was offering her a place to live, but she was paying for it with the work she accomplished. In truth, she was overpaying with all the extra cooking and canning she'd been doing. Richard closed his eyes and turned back to the hull of his boat. He guided the sandpaper across the wooden slats, careful to stay with the grain. It was imperative to have as smooth a bottom as possible. It allowed the boat's hull to cut through the waves and gain speed. As much as Richard loved sailing, he especially loved getting the most speed as possible out of his boat. His thoughts wandered to the local races at the yacht club…the sails stretched taut…the sleek boat reaching in the wind…

"Mr. Arman?"

He jumped a foot off the floor.

"I'm sorry. I didn't mean to startle you," Grace said, giggling as she held an armful of laundry. "I just wanted to say thank you again for praying for me. For putting me in touch with Mr. Greeley, extending my stay— everything. I really appreciate it."

"You're welcome." Richard continued to sand then thought better of getting dust on the clean laundry.

She paused for a moment as if she had more to say but then nodded and headed back toward the house. He closed his eyes. The woman was getting under his skin. And he didn't know if he liked it or wanted to run away screaming and get away from her. A large part of him wanted to wrap her in his arms and hold back the world. To keep her safe.

He went back to his sanding. Tomorrow he'd be applying the first layer of paint. If only fixing Grace was as easy as repairing his boat.

# Chapter 9

The next couple of days were uneventful, and Grace relished them. As she was finishing up the morning breakfast and cleaning the kitchen, there was a knock on the door. "Good morning, Mrs. Martin," a masculine voice called from behind the screen door.

"Do I know you?" Grace asked as she wiped her hands on a towel and went toward him.

"Forgive me, my name is Charles Bennett. I've come to inquire as to whether or not you might be interested in a courtship."

Grace rolled back on her heels.

"Forgive me for being so forward, but I've been petitioning your father for a year, and he's assured me that you are not available."

"Pardon?" Grace couldn't believe her ears. "For a year?"

"Yes, ma'am. I've seen you in town and in church and,

while I'm a humble man of humble means, I believe I could provide for a wife and children. However, I believe in a marriage of mutual attraction and interests. Which is why I am asking for a possible courtship."

Grace took a moment to assess him. He was handsome to look at. He had a lean build. His hands were twisting the daylights out of his felt hat. "Mr. Bennett, why are you approaching me now?"

"Your father said you had moved out and were no longer seeking his advice. So, he told me where I might find you, and I thought I should at least give it one last attempt. You won't see me beg, Mrs. Martin. I am not that kind of person. But I believe your father felt I was unworthy of your affections because I am a man of humble means."

"Mr. Bennett, please try to understand, I am honored by your interest and that you think I'm worthy of becoming your wife but..." She bent her head low and took a moment to compose her thoughts. "My life is in a bit of a chaotic state with regard to my husband's estate. I do not have the wherewithal to engage in any kind of courtship. I hope you can understand."

Charles Bennett bowed and set his crumpled hat upon his head. "I thank you for being honest, ma'am."

"You're welcome." He started to leave. "Mr. Bennett I shall pray for you to find your spouse soon."

He turned back to her. His smile spread, highlighted by long creases and cheerful eyes. "That's mighty fine of you, ma'am. Thank you. And I shall pray that you find resolution with your husband's affairs quickly."

"Thank you. I appreciate that."

"You're welcome. Good day, Mrs. Martin."

"Good day, Mr. Bennett."

Grace turned and found Richard Arman staring at her, his back rigid and his arms crossed. "Who was that?"

Fire blazed her cheeks. "A gentleman caller. Apparently, my father is telling potential suitors where I live. He is no longer fielding their inquiries."

"I take it that means we will have a constant stream of suitors coming to the inn."

Grace shrugged.

Richard mumbled. Grace couldn't figure out what he said but knew he wasn't excited about the possible disruptions. Honestly, she couldn't imagine men lining up to court her. Then again, how was she going to handle any interruptions of that sort if they did?

Later that day, she received a notice from the attorney saying that he had found a will. It would be a day or two before he would have access to it. Also, Mr. William Sears would be joining her in the lawsuit if the will left the property and all Micah's worldly possessions to his wife. Grace shook her head in bewilderment. Once she would have had no doubt of Micah's love and affection, but to keep something like this a secret from her? Why? For what purpose?

"Mrs. Martin," Richard addressed her as he entered the dining room. "What smells so wonderful this evening?" He sat down in the same seat he'd been sitting in since the first night she had shared an evening table with him.

"Pulled pork barbecue. It's really not cooked on a grill but rather slow cooked for hours. I started it last night."

"I know, and my stomach has been doing flips all day in eager anticipation. I also had to remind several of the boarders that we do not serve an evening meal."

Grace chuckled. It was nice to laugh freely.

"You think that's funny? You should hear the pleas I receive from some of the men, begging me to let them eat dinner with us. One man even offered me five dollars for dinner tonight."

Manny came in and joined them. After all, he had hunted the pig down and brought it home. "Smells mighty fine, Grace. Mighty fine. I know Richard here can cook, but it ain't nothing like you can."

Grace bowed her head, hiding a grin.

"And you're one to talk, Manny."

"Hey, I never made no claims as to being a good cook." Manny gobbled down his pork dinner. "Mighty fine dinner. Thank you, Grace."

"You're welcome." Grace looked down at her half-eaten plate then glanced over to Richard, who had eaten about half of his meal, as well.

Richard shook his head as Manny left the dining room. "The man doesn't understand the meaning of enjoying one's meal."

"I heard that. Night y'all."

Richard and Grace exchanged a smile, then his smile faded as he kept his eyes on hers. "Mrs. Martin, we should talk."


Richard took in a deep pull of air. Manny's advice that he should marry Grace rang over and over again in his mind. "I've been mulling over your situation."

Grace put down her fork and sat ramrod straight in the chair.

Richard swallowed. "And, well, mine, too. It seems to me I could provide you with some protection against all kinds of suitors as well as provide a good home and income for you."

Grace knitted her eyebrows.

"Mrs. Martin…Grace." He calmed his nerves and reached for her hand. "I'm not good with women. I made a terrible mess of my previous relationship and well…I know I'm not offering love and roses. But I think a business arrangement would work between us."

"What?" Grace squeaked.

"Hear me out. See, I know you are in need of a permanent dwelling, and I know you do not want to get married again. I thought that since you're so good with the upkeep of the inn, wonderful with the customers and such a fine cook, perhaps it might make sense to avoid rumors and any sense of impropriety by getting married. You would be part owner of the Seaside Inn, as well."

Grace sat back in her seat. "So you're proposing a business arrangement, a marriage of convenience."

"Yes, exactly." Richard gave a half smile. He still wasn't certain how she was reacting. "I know this has come out of the blue, but I've been thinking about it on and off since you moved in. I do not want your reputation soiled. I'm a reasonably good-looking man, and I'm not asking for any marriage favors. In fact, I've given this a lot of thought. You could move into my room and I'd sleep in another. No one would be the wiser. Perhaps Manny would figure it out, but certainly not our guests."

"Not a real marriage."

"A legal marriage, with all the rights a wife would be entitled to. If something were to happen to me, you will inherit the inn. You can run it or sell it, whatever you choose." He hoped he wasn't pleading. "You would be my wife in every other way."

"What if our desires should change one day?"

"If you fall in love with another, I would give you an annulment if that is what you wished."

Grace bowed her head and looked into her lap. "No," she whispered. "What if you desired to have all the rights of a real husband?"

"Oh. Well, I don't foresee.... What I mean is, you're attractive and all but I would never presume myself upon you. I give my word that I will be a perfect gentleman. Also, as your husband, I'd be able to help you with your legal issues."

"Would Micah's land become yours?"

"No. I'm not interested in Micah's land. That will be yours free and clear. You can do whatever you wish with the property." Richard paused. "Grace, I know I am not the kind of man women find themselves wanting. If you can see past that, I believe we could have a wonderful working relationship as well as a respectful friendship. I've enjoyed our dinners together. They have become the highlight of my day." He paused, but she didn't say anything.

"I would look forward to sharing with you about the business and asking for your input. Don't forget, the Seaside was run by my grandmother for many years. I am not a man who believes a woman has no say. I would honor you and seek your counsel. I have found you to be an incredible woman of impeccable character, and I would be honored to call you my wife."

Grace smiled. She reached over and patted the top of his hand. "No, I don't believe that would be a good relationship for us."

Richard nodded. "Very well. But if you should change your mind, the offer stands." He stood up. "Dinner was exceptional as always, but I believe I have had my fill. It is my night to clean up. When you're finished, just leave your dishes on the table and I'll take care of them."

"Richard, wait. I didn't mean to offend you."

"No offense taken. It was a thought, perhaps not a great one. As I said, I have difficulty relating to women."

"Now who told you such a foolish thing?" Grace asked.

Richard sat back down. "My fiancée. Nothing I did was good enough for her. Grandmother said it was her, but Grandmother never knew Willa Jean."

"Well, I have to agree with your grandmother. You have been nothing but a gentleman to me. You've shown me more compassion and sensitivity than any man I've known, and that includes my husband, Micah."

A spark of hope ignited deep in his chest. Could there be a chance for Grace and him to have a real relationship?

"I don't see the need to get married. I think our arrangement has been working so far."

"Absolutely. I was more concerned about your being asked to court over and over again. You are a beautiful woman, and I know the line of suitors will be a fairly lengthy one."

Grace smiled. "You think I'm beautiful?"

Richard shook his head. "I'm not committing to anything. Ask any man here, and they will all tell you that you are a beautiful woman. That's all I'm saying. I'm not suggesting…" He was burying himself deeper. "It's just a business arrangement, Grace. Nothing more, nothing less. And if I do say so myself, a very generous offer."

"What about children? I mean if we're not…you know. How would you feel not having any children of your own?"

"I've done just fine without any so far," Richard

teased. Even so, an image of Grace heavy with child filled his imagination. And a desire to have children was planted in the back of his mind.

"Having children is only one of the matters we would need to discuss—if I were to agree to such a thing."

Richard's heart lightened. "Ask me any questions you like. To you, I will be an open book."

"Tell me more about Willa Jean."

Richard proceeded to tell of the hurt and betrayal he felt from Willa Jean and all her nonsense, and how his grandmother had helped him get past a lot of the pain and rejection. "I know I'm not great husband material."

"No, Richard. You are not what *Willa Jean* was looking for in a husband. And from what you have said about her, I doubt any man could fill those boots. She wanted a man who would buy her anything and spend his undivided time and attention on her, but only when she wanted it. Marriage is more than that."

"I know. But I can't see how I could ever find a person who would want to be with me, and only me, for the rest of her life."

"You sell yourself short, Richard. You are a handsome man, easy on the eyes. You also have such a compassionate heart. I've seen you dealing with customers in such a personal way. You're a good businessman. No question your goal is to pay your bills and make a profit, which is a good thing, but you also give when and where you can."

Richard nodded. His throat was too thick to speak.

Grace's hands stopped shaking. Richard had asked her to marry him. Her attraction to him doubled in that very moment. She wouldn't mind being married to him. On the other hand, was she really ready for another marriage? After all that had transpired, she wasn't certain. "Richard, the truth is I said no because I feel you deserve more than a marriage of convenience."

"And you need to know you, too, are an incredible person. As I said, I truly would be honored," he said softly.

"Thank you." Perhaps they did have hope of having a real relationship. Was she ready for that? To share her heart, her dreams and a future with him? After all, she was only twenty-three. "How old are you?" she bumbled out.

"Twenty-seven. You?"

"Twenty-three." She worried her lower lip as she forked through the food on her plate. She wasn't very hungry any longer.

Richard stood up again. "One more thing about getting married. We'd be free to call each other by our first names at the inn." Richard winked and carried his plates to the kitchen.

He didn't fight fair.

Grace did as he asked and left her dishes on the table. Tonight she could have gotten lost in his greenish-blue eyes. And a stray thought of running her fingers through his hair surprised her. If her interest in him continued to rise, a platonic marriage would be out of the question.

The next morning Grace woke with a groan. Sleep had eluded her most of the night, the remainder plagued with dreams and nightmares. During those night terrors, pleasant memories of Micah and their relationship would disintegrate into a nightmare where Micah transformed into a man she didn't recognize, and she was surrounded by people chasing her. Some of the people in her dreams wanted to marry her, others wanted Micah's land, and

Micah's family hovered over her as large, angry, distorted faces. Grace threw off the covers and shuddered at the retreating images.

She stumbled into the kitchen and prepared the bacon and sausages. Today she'd serve a light fare with pancakes, eggs, toast and jam along with the breakfast meats.

Richard strode into the kitchen. "Good morning, Mrs. Martin." He walked past as if the conversation they'd had the night before had never happened.

"Good morning, Mr. Arman. Is there anything you'd like me to prepare this morning?"

"I trust your judgment. We've had a couple more sign up for breakfast. You can expect thirteen this morning."

"Thank you." Thirteen plus Richard, herself and Manny. Those three, she'd learned, were a given.

Richard nodded and exited the kitchen. Had she offended him by rejecting his marriage proposal? But it wasn't a real marriage proposal, was it? It was a business arrangement, and admittedly she wanted more. On the other hand, she wasn't prepared for more. Richard was a handsome man but there was…she paused. His words from last night circled through her mind once again. She couldn't believe Willa Jean had been so, so…what was the right word? Abusive? No, that wasn't it. A manipulative, self-centered person seemed to describe her best.

Manny came in through the back door. "Mornin', Grace. How are you today?"

"Fine, thank you, and you?"

"Been feeling a bit poorly." Manny coughed. "I won't be eating this morning, just a cup of tea." He sniffed the air. "Bacon sure smells good, though." Manny ran his palm gently across his stomach. "Probably not." He poured himself a cup of hot water from the kettle then set some tea leaves in his cup. "I'll be in my room," he muttered and exited the kitchen with the mug in his hands.

He did appear a bit pale this morning, Grace mused. She'd never known anything to keep the man from food.

A couple of hours later the meal was done and she was washing the remaining dishes when Richard came in again. "Did you see Manny this morning?"

"Yes. He said he wasn't feeling well and took a cup of tea to his room."

"I'll go check on him."

Grace nodded and continued to wash the dishes. As she was drying off the last plate and putting it back in the cupboard, Richard returned. "He said he's fine, just not up to par. He said that behind a closed door. I hate to think what that room looks like, but that's how it's been since long before I came here."

She turned and faced him, dish towel in hand. Before she could speak, a tremendous crack of thunder rattled the entire inn. She and Richard flew toward the window. Dark, rolling clouds boiled around them as large drops of rain bounced off the windowsill. "I guess I won't be doing the laundry today."

"Doesn't appear so. Perhaps it will be a fast-moving storm, though."

"Perhaps," she said, her voice distant. All she could sense at the moment was his presence at her side, strong and comforting. Nervous tension filled the air. "Richard, I'm sorry."

He turned and leaned against the countertop. "Grace, I am not hurt or offended. I hope I didn't offend you by extending such an offer."

She bowed her head and shook it. "No, I was not offended."

"But you're still hoping for romantic love."

She raised her gaze and caught his lively blue-green eyes and smiled. "Yes, I guess I am."

He crossed his arms. "Grace, I am not a romantic man. And while I would—" he cleared his throat "—want a real marriage, I've come to accept that is not a part of my future."

She reached over and touched his lips with her finger. They were warm, soft.... She removed her finger. "Richard, I do not wish to hear you put yourself down in such a manner again. You are far more than you believe yourself to be."

She stepped away and walked toward the stove, across the room from where he stood. "I'll do it," she said, keeping her back to him. "I'll marry you."

# Chapter 10

Richard couldn't believe his ears. "Are you certain?"

"Yes, under one condition."

"Anything, absolutely anything." He needed to calm down. As much as he would love a wife one day, this was a business arrangement. A pleasant business arrangement but still business.

"That if one day you decide you have feelings of love for me, you will tell me."

Richard's eyes widened. He already had feelings of love, though he wasn't certain he could tell her. He nodded.

She nodded. "Good, then we are agreed. When should we marry?"

"As soon as possible, I suppose. Do you want a fancy wedding?" He hoped she wouldn't. Not because of the expense, he told himself, but this was a private matter.

"No, nothing like that. I'm thinking you and me and a minister."

His heart lightened. They were in agreement. "I believe there will need to be a witness or two."

"Right." She nodded and paced. "How about Manny?"

Richard chuckled. "Manny would do." Richard stepped over to her. "I know this may sound silly but your accepting my proposal has made me a very happy man. I'll move my belongings into your room, and you can move into mine. I'll still need to go in there to work on the office material for the inn, though."

"I can stay in my room."

"No, no, I insist you take the larger room. You're going to be the best business partner a man ever had."

She wagged her head. "Thank you."

"As I said, Mrs. Martin. Hmm… I suppose you'll be Mrs. Arman from now on."

Grace's eyes widened.

*Did she not want to take his name?* He couldn't allow his heart to think that way. She was a woman trapped in her circumstances. He was giving her a future. She would be an incredible asset to the Seaside and to him personally. He prayed they would find a helpmate in each other one day.

"I hadn't thought about that. Sorry, you are correct. I will be called Mrs. Arman after we are married. When, do you think?"

Richard hesitated. He wanted to say now. Why wait? On the other hand, this was a business relationship, and he should keep it professional. "How about Wednesday? It's in the middle of the week, fewer clients. Do you want to invite guests? Your parents?"

"My parents…" Her words trailed off. She thought for a moment. "No, they would not approve. We will have to tell them eventually but…"

Richard came up beside her. "I'll take care of them." He looked down into her deep brown eyes. He wanted to caress her face, to push all her cares away like the strands of hair lying across her face. "I'll visit with them later today and let them know."

Grace blinked then paused with her eyelids closed. "Thank you. I don't believe I could bear hearing Father's accusations. Prepare yourself. He will not be thrilled because he did not plan this."

"I can handle your father, Grace." He reached out and placed his hands on her shoulders. "Trust me to take care of you."

"I do. And Richard, trust me to take care of you, as well."

He smiled, his heart racing, and her lips parted in a joyful response. "I do."

Wednesday morning came so quickly. Grace had fed the boarders and finished cleaning the kitchen when Richard entered wearing one of his fancy outfits. She felt terribly underdressed. She hadn't seen these clothes before; at least she didn't believe so. "Let me change," she said, tearing off her apron on her way out of the kitchen.

"We have an hour before the pastor is expecting us."

"Good. I will need every minute of it."

Manny walked in, a bit pale but wearing a big, toothless grin. "I told ya to marry her."

Grace groaned. Manny was an interesting character. He'd been holed up in his room for the past couple of days, coming out for an occasional tea. Grace was glad to see him on his feet and willing to be their witness.

Richard had informed her parents, and their response had been as she expected. Her father was not interested in hearing of her plans. Instead he belittled Richard with words she could only imagine. Richard had refused to talk about what he'd said. She'd been right, her father found him to be lacking in the husband department. She didn't have a clue who her father thought would be the perfect husband for her, but she was certain it had nothing to do with the love or mutual admiration she and Richard had for one another. There was no denying the lack of romantic love in their relationship, but they were quickly becoming best friends. And isn't that what a couple wants in their marriage? Isn't that what Mercy Hastings had found in her relationship with Wyatt?

The love part she was content to leave behind. She had loved Micah, and that hadn't helped her much. Richard was a strong, stable man with a heart of compassion. She hurried into her room, her thoughts on Micah. Mr. Greeley had obtained a copy of the will. The property had been left to her, but there was no mention of why he had hidden the purchase from her. There was certainly nothing to explain why her in-laws thought they would keep the property for themselves—apart from the obvious: they were already using the land for their cattle.

Grace chose a simple spring dress with a blue skirt and a white top with blue ribboning. It had long sleeves and cuffs made from the same blue material as the skirt. She repinned her hair up in a bun, over which she placed a small hat. She brushed on some face powder. Richard might be wanting a businesslike arranged marriage, but she wanted people in town to believe she was an asset to him.

Coming to terms with this arrangement had taken several days. And while she wasn't ready to commit to him as a wife in every way as she had to Micah, she was willing to commit to him and the Seaside Inn in a partnership. Together they would make it a comfortable place for others to stay while in town. She scanned the large master bedroom, her room. She still could not believe it. Sitting in the corner was Richard's desk. She thought at first it would be difficult knowing he would be in the room on a regular basis, but so far it worked. In some odd way she felt his presence even when she was alone in the room, and that presence made her feel calm and secure. It wasn't the best way to marry a man but, for now, it felt like the right way. She examined herself in the mirror and headed out the door.

Richard placed his finger between his neck and collar, stretching it for a bit more breathing room. The starched collar did nothing to ease his discomfort. He had spent more time praying over the past week than he had in a long time. He felt certain he was doing the right thing. At the very least he was providing Grace protection. He pulled his pocket watch out. One-thirty. They still had half an hour before they were due to meet the pastor at the parsonage.

Grace stepped into the room. Richard couldn't believe his eyes. "You look beautiful."

A pink blush rose on her cheeks. "Thank you," she whispered. "You're looking handsome, as well."

Richard cleared his throat. This was not the kind of discussion they should continue, considering the platonic marriage they had agreed to. "Shall we?" he asked, extending an elbow.

"Are you certain? You seem to be giving up everything and getting little in return."

"Nonsense. You're an incredible asset to the Seaside."

Richard paused. "And to me," he whispered. He wasn't certain she heard his response. He hoped she didn't. There was no sense having her think he would like a real marriage when he had agreed to a platonic one. Maybe in a year or two after they got to know one another better, perhaps then he could do as she asked and share his heart. But not now. Now she needed security. She needed to know she had value just for who she was, not because of who her parents were or who her husband was, but simply for being Grace.

Manny met them at the bottom of the steps with the carriage. "I'll ride with you to the reverend's house, but after the ceremony I'll be heading out for a bit with my buddies."

No doubt Manny wanted to give them some time alone and privacy, Richard realized, not understanding the type of marriage he and Grace would be sharing. Soon enough he would.

Richard assisted her into the carriage and sat beside her. Manny stood outside on the boot at the rear. Richard picked up the reins. The carriage bucked forward as they headed toward the parsonage to meet with the pastor.

Grace wrung her gloved hands. He placed a hand on hers. "It's going to be all right. But you can bow out if you're not ready."

She looked at him. "I don't know if I'd ever be ready, but I'm still content with our arrangement. I'm just nervous."

"Very well." He removed his hand and regretted it. There was a connection he felt with her every time they touched. Maybe in a year he could share his heart with her. Richard swallowed and continued leading the wagon to the one spot in town that would change his life forever.

And yet he was happy to join himself with this woman. She was beautiful, intelligent, a good worker and she'd make a wonderful mother one… The thought stuck in his throat. Was he really hoping to have children with Grace one day? *Father God, help me be a man of my word.*

The rest of the drive to the parsonage, the moments speaking with the pastor before the service all vanished with two sentences: "Congratulations, Mr. and Mrs. Arman. You may now kiss the bride." Richard leaned back on his heels. They had never talked about that part of the ceremony. In truth, they hadn't talked much at all about the ceremony. Richard paused for a moment then leaned forward and gave Grace a quick little peck on the lips.

The pastor's face drooped.

Grace gazed into Richard's eyes and smiled. The pastor smiled with relief.

Richard signed the paperwork and paid the pastor for his services. Grace reached for the crook of her husband's elbow and held on. He placed a hand on top of hers.

Manny came up and slapped his back. "Well, it's about time. I'll see you later. Congratulations, Mrs. Arman." He winked at Grace.

"Thank you, Manny."

They were back in the carriage before she asked, "What did Manny mean by *it's about time?*"

Richard chuckled. "He's been suggesting I marry you since you came to work for me. I think he prefers your cooking over mine."

"Well, that's possible, I suppose. What is the story behind Manny? How long has he been living at the inn? Where'd he come from? Who's his family?"

Richard flicked the reins, and the horse started out at

a slow pace. "I don't know much. Grandmother said he was an old friend of my grandfather's. She treated him like a brother, more or less. He has a special rate for his room that my grandmother set. He's responsible for his own linens, as you know, but I honestly have never been allowed in his room. He always meets me in the hall or talks behind a closed door. As for his family, well, I don't believe he has any. You and I are it."

Grace chuckled. "So I just adopted an eccentric uncle?"

"That's a good way to put it. By the way, I sent a letter to my parents to say that I was getting married. They know nothing of the details about our arrangement, but I felt they should know."

"It's only fair but..."

Richard waited for her response.

"Shouldn't they know the truth?"

"No. Because my parents would think you were after my assets. They need to meet you and get to know you before I tell them the truth. And even then I may not. Our arrangement is personal between the two of us, and I'd like to keep it that way. I believe it will protect us both against false innuendo and gossip."

"You're probably right. I'm certain once the Martins hear I've married, they'll say I don't need the land."

Richard wrapped his arm around Grace. She leaned in and placed her head upon his shoulder. He liked how comfortable she felt in his arms. "I will not tell you what to do concerning the property, but if you want advice, I'm willing to listen."

"I appreciate that."

"Now, I would like to take you out to dinner tonight in honor of our marriage. Where would you like to go?"

* * *

Several hours later Grace found herself in her room, alone. The difference between her first wedding night and her second...well, she wouldn't venture down that path. It had been hard enough not to kiss him back during the wedding ceremony. He'd been the perfect gentleman during dinner. He had presented her as his wife. He was attentive to her needs and desires. A woman couldn't ask for more. It was an honor to be Mrs. Richard Arman. She went over to his desk and ran her finger over the smooth oak chair. She'd seen him sitting here twice now, and she liked it.

A soft shuffle of feet in the hallway caught her attention, followed by a gentle tap on the door. "Grace," Richard whispered.

She opened the door. "What's the matter?"

"Forgive me, but I forgot to pack my housecoat. It's hanging on a peg on the back of the closet door."

Grace opened the door. "Come in." She stepped back.

He stepped into the room. "I'm so sorry."

"Nonsense, we are sharing a name." Perhaps not the room but then again they were sharing it, in a manner of speaking. Her cheeks flamed as she shut down that train of thought.

"Thank you. I'll be quick." Richard went over to the closet, opened the door and pulled his housecoat off the peg.

She followed every move he made. Did she truly trust him? She was his wife. He would have every right to demand his... No, that was not Richard, and that was not their arrangement.

"Richard?"

He turned and faced her. "Yes?"

"I just wanted to thank you again for—" she paused "—for everything you've been doing for me. You've been a perfect gentleman and a good friend."

"I believe our friendship will continue to grow, Grace, and I'm looking forward to that."

"Me, too," she admitted.

"Good night, Grace."

"Good night, Richard." And with that, he slipped out the door and down the hall. He was a man of honor, and that was something she should never question.

Grace made herself ready for bed and slipped into the first peaceful night's sleep since before she'd left her parents' home.

By the end of their first week of marriage, Grace found a rhythm in working with Richard and responding to being called Mrs. Arman.

"Good morning, Mrs. Arman." Rudy, one of the young sailors who had found his way to the inn, greeted her as she refreshed his coffee.

"Good morning, Rudy. Did you sleep well?"

"Yes, ma'am. Thank you for breakfast. I haven't eaten this well since my ma last cooked for me."

"Pleasure to be at your service. Have a great day."

"Yes, ma'am. Mr. Arman is a mighty lucky fellow marrying someone so pretty and who can cook like you." Rudy winked.

Richard walked in and glared at Rudy, who returned the look with an innocent smile. "I was just telling your wife…"

"I heard what you were telling my wife."

"Oh, well, as I was telling her, you're a lucky man."

"That I am, Rudy." Richard pulled out his pocket watch. "Tide's just about full."

Rudy bolted up from his chair. "See you next time, Mr. and Mrs. Arman."

Grace chuckled. Richard turned toward her. "I don't know if it is wise to be so comfortable with the guests."

"Oh, Richard, he's just a boy and perfectly harmless." Grace gathered up a few dishes and headed into the kitchen.

"Perhaps."

She turned and faced him. "Richard, you're not afraid I would…"

"No, no, nothing like that." He walked up beside her. "Our customers are not always of the highest caliber. I wouldn't want any of them expressing the wrong intentions."

Grace smiled. "And I foolishly thought you might be jealous." She winked.

Richard groaned.

"Please give me a hand in the kitchen. I would like to speak with you for a few moments."

Richard grabbed a few more dishes from the table and followed her into the kitchen. She carried her armful in from the dining room and placed it on the counter. Richard did the same then started to scrape the dishes clean, putting the leftovers in the barrel for the compost pile. Grace pumped some water into the sink and pulled the pot from the stove. "I've been thinking about our customers," she said, amazed at how comfortable she felt calling them her customers as well as his. "And I was wondering if we're making a profit off the breakfasts."

"I've been charging them a dollar. Then most of the men pay for seconds. I've even had a couple pay me a dollar fifty. Then there are the occasional ones who can't afford to pay, and I can tell they're down on their luck, so I let them have a complimentary breakfast."

"Like Joe yesterday?"

"Yes. How'd you know?"

"Joe had that disheveled look like he'd been up all night playing cards and drinking."

"You're probably right." Richard stacked the plates by the sink.

Grace poured the pot of hot water into the sink. "Speaking of someone a bit down on his luck—Manny didn't come out for breakfast again this morning."

"I noticed that, too. I'll check on him in a minute. Was the price of the breakfast what you wanted to speak with me about this morning?"

"Yes and no." How could she say this without giving him the wrong impression? "I thought it might be nice if we could spend some time together." There, she said it. She prayed he wouldn't think her too forward.

"I was planning on putting the finishing touches on my boat today. I'm hoping to launch it later this week."

"Can I help?" she asked. "I'll try not to get in the way."

Richard came up beside her and wrapped her in his embrace. "Of course you can help, Mrs. Arman."

She closed her eyes and relished the limited intimacy they shared. There had been nothing but a few embraces since they married, but she so loved being wrapped in his arms. She felt safe, secure, and all her troubles seemed to melt away.

"Let me check in on Manny, and then after lunch we'll work in the barn together."

"I'd like that."

Richard gently released her, and she went back to washing the dishes. They were miles away from becoming husband and wife in the true sense of the word, but she cherished the friendship that was developing between the two of them.

The dishes done and the beds stripped and remade, she went to work washing the linens. A delivery truck with a large crate on the back end pulled up to the rear of the house.

She marched up to the deliveryman. "How can I help you?"

"A delivery for the Seaside Inn. Sign here, please."

Grace accepted the clipboard and signed on the appropriate line. "What is this?"

The service man shrugged. Richard came out the back door with a crowbar in hand. "Oh, good, it's here."

"What's here?" Grace asked.

"I bought you a little something."

"Me?"

Richard and the deliveryman lowered the crate. Richard shoved the crowbar between the crate's slats, opening it up to the sound of pulled nails and splintering wood.

"A washing machine?"

## Chapter 11

Richard sat at his desk sorting through the various bills and receipts. A smile formed at the memory of Grace's reaction to the delivery of the washing machine. Having one at the inn made Grace's workload a lot lighter. It also allowed her to spend more time with him, and Richard loved how close they were becoming.

"Grace?" he called out. A letter from his attorney addressed to her meant something was developing with her case.

Grace came into the bedroom. She was dressed in a lovely pale green dress this morning. "What do you need?"

"There's a letter here from Mr. Greeley."

Grace came forward, opened it and scanned the pages. "We have a court date." Her hands began to tremble.

"What's the matter?"

"They're trying to deny Micah's will, claiming he told

them the land was for them if anything was to happen to him."

"That is the opposite of what Micah's will said, correct?"

"Yes. Micah's will stated that I was his sole heir, and I was to use it to provide for myself in the event he didn't survive the war." A faraway look accompanied her fading voice.

Richard nodded and stood up. "Grace, tell me what else is troubling you."

"I'm sorry. It brings up so much. Those last couple of days we shared together were so romantic, and I thought we were so close. But he never told me about this land. I don't understand why." She began to pace. He came up behind her and placed his hands on her shoulders.

She turned in his arms. Richard closed his eyes and relished the closeness they shared with one another. He was always careful not to overstep his bounds, but he knew she enjoyed their embraces as much as he did. "I'm so angry with them, I don't want to see them. And this trial…"

"Grace," he said and lifted her chin. "You can ask Mr. Greeley to represent you. You don't have to appear in court, unless the Martins' attorney calls you to be a witness. Which I doubt they would."

"I just wish this entire mess would go away." She stepped out of his embrace. "I'll go to Mr. Greeley's office later today and sign the paperwork he mentioned in the letter. It was wrong for the Martins to keep this land from me. And while I still don't know why Micah owed Mr. Sears the money, I really don't care anymore. I want this entire matter to end."

Richard went back to his desk. "It will. I know Mr.

Greeley is working on it and expediting the matter quickly."

She nodded. "I better get back to the dusting."

"And I to the bookwork. I'd be happy to accompany you to the lawyer's, if you would like."

She paused at the doorway and sighed. "It's my problem, I'll take care of it."

"I understand. But if you change your mind, I'm happy to come along."

"Thank you. I appreciate all you've done for me. Oh, and can I just say thank you again for the washing machine? What a marvelous invention."

"I'm glad you like it." He sat down. His love for Grace was growing each day, and this distraction from work was a welcome interruption.

"What a time-saver. I heard of such things but never in my wildest dreams thought I'd own one. The clothes dry quicker with the wringer squeezing out all the water. Since it's spring, may I suggest we start cleaning all the bedspreads and comforters?"

"Yes. I forgot about those." Several items had been forgotten since Grace started to work for him. Even more since they married. Richard reached for the book where he kept a seasonal to-do list.

"Wonderful. I'll begin today with the empty rooms. Where do we store the winter quilts?"

"In the back of the linen closet is a cubby where winter and spring items are kept. I'll show you." Richard started to get up.

"Sit. You can show me later."

Richard scooted the chair over and sat back down.

Grace slipped out of the room and closed the door behind her. In the past when he worked alone, he had kept the door open in order to hear what was going on at the inn. Now, with Grace as his partner, he had the freedom to keep the door closed and allow himself to concentrate. And while he was forgetting some of the items on the yearly to-do list, his workload had been easing up. "Perhaps too much," Richard chuckled to himself and went back over the bills.

His debt caused by Jorge was paid in full, and his bank account was almost back to the place it had been before Jorge's deception. Jorge's case was simple. He had pleaded no contest, and the judge sentenced him to make restitution. Richard didn't expect to see any of those funds returned. And, judging by what Sheriff Bower had turned up, Richard had no doubt Jorge would flee as soon as possible. Sheriff Bower was keeping a watch over outgoing ships and trains but knew it would be quite easy to escape unnoticed. He did have an artist come by the jail and sketch a picture of Jorge to distribute to other law enforcers if Jorge did try to escape.

Richard filed the necessary paperwork and closed his ledgers, putting them away in the various cubbies of his desk. His grandfather had built the desk specifically for managing the accounts of the inn.

Next stop was Manny's room. He hadn't come out of his room yesterday, but he did say he was fine. It didn't bode well that he was staying in his room day and night and not eating very much.

Richard knocked on Manny's door and waited. No response. He knocked again. Again, there was no response. "Manny," Richard called out with a louder knock.

Grace came around the corner.

Richard banged on the door, rattling it in its hinges. His pulse quickened.

"Richard?" Grace wrung the dishcloth in her hands.

Richard slammed his shoulder against the door. It didn't budge. "Grace, would you get me a hammer and a screwdriver?"

"Sure." She ran off.

Richard continued calling Manny's name, drawing the attention of other boarders. *Dear God, I hope he's not dead.*

Grace ran out to the barn and gathered the tools Richard asked for. Finding them on the pegboard in Richard's work area was easy. She'd been spending a fair amount of time helping him with his boat, which was nearly ready to launch. She grabbed the wooden handle of the hammer with her right hand and pulled a screwdriver down with her left. Tucking the metal shaft of the screwdriver up against her forearm, she ran back to the house and down the hall to Manny's room where she found Richard on his knees. "Thanks." He reached out for the tools.

Richard went straight to work loosening the door's cast-iron plate chipping old paint off the screw heads. In no time, he had the screws out, the doorknob and plate off. Using the screwdriver, he moved the lock and opened the door. Manny was lying on top of his bed, fully clothed. Grace rushed in. Maneuvering over piles and piles of stuff, she worked her way to his bedside.

"Manny!" she called out, and placed a finger in front of his nose. "He's breathing!"

"Good." Richard scanned the room. "I'll get the doc. Open a window."

Manny was in a corner room and should have two windows. Finding one, she opened it. Grace looked around.

At first glance she wondered if everything he owned was stuffed in this room. It would make sense, since he'd been living there for years. She left Manny and went to the kitchen, grabbed a towel and pumped some water on it. He hadn't felt warm, but perhaps a cool compress would help. "It certainly couldn't hurt," she mumbled and headed back to Manny's bedside.

Richard made room for her as she sat on the edge of the bed and applied the cloth. "Manny," she called. Again, no response. She reached out and shook his arm. "Manny, wake up, please."

Manny's eyes rolled under his lids.

"Come on, Manny, you can do it. Wake up, Manny. Come on," Grace encouraged. "Please wake up."

Manny moaned.

"That's it, Manny, fight it. Wake up." Grace removed the cool cloth, folded it over again and replaced it on his forehead.

Heavy footfalls in the hallway caused her to glance over to the doorway. Dr. Peck marched in dressed in his black suit and carrying his doctor's bag. Richard stood in the doorway.

"He's starting to wake up. He moaned a bit." Grace pulled the cloth off Manny's forehead.

"Thank you, Mrs. Martin. I'll take it from here," Dr. Peck said. "Mr. Arman, would you assist me for a moment."

"Certainly."

Grace knew it wasn't a case of not wanting a woman underfoot but rather a case of propriety. She weaved her way through the twisted path of clutter to the door. "I'll be in earshot."

"Thank you," Richard whispered, then proceeded back into the room.

"Help me remove his coat and shoes," the doctor instructed.

Grace took a step away from the door and turned her back on the three men. "Mrs. Martin," Dr. Peck called. "Would you be so kind as to make some tea?"

"Yes, sir." She wanted to correct the doctor as to her proper name, but now didn't seem the right time. Perhaps later, after his initial exam. In the kitchen she heated the water and set the teapot up with a tea ball and filled it with English breakfast tea leaves. It was a mild tea and one she found particularly pleasant in the mornings.

She returned to Manny's room and found the doctor listening to his chest. Richard turned and gave her a nod, which meant Manny was doing better. She soon heard the whistle of the teakettle on the stove and returned to the kitchen. Making quick work of filling the teapot and placing a saucer and teacup on a tray with the teapot, she returned to Manny's room. "Tea is ready."

"Thank you, Mrs. Martin," Dr. Peck said without turning his attention to her, and continued his examination of Manny.

"Mrs. Arman," she corrected.

Dr. Peck turned and looked at Grace then back to Richard. "Forgive me, I didn't know. Congratulations."

"It was a small wedding," Richard answered, and came to her side, taking the tray from her. "We'll take it from here." He leaned into her. "I think he'll need to go to the hospital for a few days," he whispered.

"Is he going to be all right?"

"Don't know yet. Doc will take care of him. I'm going to help him change Manny. His clothes are soiled."

Grace flushed. "I'll wash his clothes and bedding."

"Thank you." He kissed her cheek.

Grace's heart raced.

"I'll speak with you before we leave to take him to the hospital. Can you handle the front desk?"

Grace nodded. "Yes." She'd never done it before, but she'd watched Richard register guests many times. It couldn't be that difficult.

"Thank you. Once Manny's settled in the hospital, I'll return."

"I'll have dinner ready."

He slipped into the room. "Thank you," he said one more time as he pulled the door shut.

Grace stepped back. She felt like a fish out of water. She wanted to help but knew she couldn't. She went to her room and changed from her cleaning clothes to a more presentable dress for greeting potential customers. At the front desk, she looked over the register and noted which rooms were occupied and which were available for guests.

"I'm fine," Manny mumbled.

Grace turned to see Richard holding Manny up. "We're heading to the hospital."

"Do you know what's ailing him, Doctor?"

"Dehydration, I fear," Dr. Peck answered. "In the hospital we can provide around the clock nursing, encouraging him to drink as much as possible."

"I'm fine," Manny mumbled again.

Grace walked over to him and wrapped him in a hug. "Go to the hospital, Manny. Do it for me. I'm worried about you."

Manny raised his head and nodded. "For you, Grace. I'll do it for you."

"Thank you." She hugged him again then stepped away.

"I'll be back as soon as possible," Richard said.

Grace nodded.

* * *

Richard arrived back at the inn a few hours later, weary and hungry. He was overwhelmed by Grace's compassion for Manny and her understanding of what he meant to him. Not that Richard would ever admit it, but he'd grown to love the odd old man. It was like Grace said, he was an eccentric uncle nobody really claimed but all in the family loved. And yet he wasn't family, not real family. But Manny had been there for his grandmother. He'd helped around the inn, encouraging her and brightening her day when no one else, including himself, had been able to.

He'd take care of Manny and his medical expenses. It was the least he could do. So much for catching up on his bills, Richard thought with a chuckle as he pulled the front door of the inn open. A group of men had gathered in the sitting room. Grace was in the center and all seemed to be engaged in light laughter. "Richard!" Grace jumped up when she spotted him. "How is he?"

"He's going to be fine. Dr. Peck says he'll be in the hospital for a couple of days. Once he's past the worst of it, he'll let him come home."

"Come, join us. I've been talking with these fine young men and they are willing to help us clean Manny's room tomorrow. Isn't that wonderful?"

"Yes, thank you." No, he wanted to protest, you can't just throw away Manny's things. But now was not the time.

"I thought that we could organize his belongings and put everything in crates. Then we could store them against a back wall in the barn. What do you think? Would that take away from your workshop?"

Richard breathed a sigh of relief. She was only trying to help. "Where would we get all the crates?"

"I delivered fifteen to the grocer this morning," one of the sailors said. "I went by there this evening and asked if I could have the empty crates, and the owner said it wouldn't be a problem."

"And I got a couple of barrels from Capt. Jefferies," Evan Stanley spoke up.

"It's good to see you again, Mr. Stanley."

"It's good to be back. I have two days in port, so I'm more than willing to lend a hand," Evan answered.

Grace smiled. "Isn't it wonderful, Mr. Arman?"

"Yes, it is, Mrs. Arman." He smiled back. "Forgive me men, but I haven't eaten…."

The sailors all jumped up. "Not a problem, Mr. Arman. Your missus was saying you'd be hungry. We'll get out of your way. We'll all be ready after breakfast tomorrow to get a start on Manny's room."

"Thank you all. I believe Manny will be grateful for your help."

"Good night," the sailors called out, and left the sitting area. Some headed down the hall and others up the stairs.

"Well, you've been busy," Richard snickered.

"That I have, husband. I started by stripping the bed and washing all the clothes I could find. I'm certain there is a lot more. I'm also certain there are a lot of things we could throw away and Manny would not be the wiser. However, I suspect he likes his things, even the ones he's forgotten about."

Richard chuckled and draped his arm across Grace's shoulders. "Of that, my dear wife, I am certain."

"Tell me what happened at the hospital and what is wrong with Manny."

Richard let her know that it appeared that Manny simply hadn't had enough fluids but the doctor was running further tests. "Apparently, Manny's solution to the runs was to stop eating altogether. Dr. Peck told him that he was putting Manny on a black tea, white rice diet for a couple of days to see if that would fix his problem."

They went into the kitchen together and served themselves their evening meal and sat down in the dining area. "Did you have any trouble registering the new boarders?"

"No, not at all. I've watched you enough."

"Good. I felt you could handle it, but I should have shown you how to do it ages ago. I'm sorry. Let's pray." Richard took Grace's hand. He loved the fact that they now sat beside each other. Grace had changed her seat after they married. "Father, thank You for helping us save Manny. We ask Your continued healing on his body, and help him not be upset about the changes that will be coming to his room. He can't live like that. Help us to say the right words and not offend him."

"Amen," Grace said, and picked up her fork. "Richard, I love your heart of compassion."

Richard felt the right side of his lips curl. "Thank you. I love your compassionate heart, as well. Obviously, we've adopted that old man." Richard chuckled.

"Obviously," Grace giggled. He loved the lilt of her laughter.

A knock on the dining room door frame interrupted their meal. Richard glanced up to see Sheriff Bower, his hat in his hands. "Mr. Arman, we have a problem."

# Chapter 12

"Shall I leave?" Grace asked, putting her fork down on her plate.

"No, Mrs. Arman, this concerns you, as well."

"What seems to be the problem, Sheriff?" Richard asked. He placed his hand on top of hers.

"May I sit?" Sheriff Bower motioned toward an empty seat at the table.

"Certainly." Richard stood up and pulled out the chair then returned to his seat.

"Rumors are beginning to surface about Jorge. Some say he's left town. Others say he wants revenge on you, Richard."

"Ah. And how much danger am I in?"

"I don't believe Jorge is of the mind-set to physically hurt you, but he could try to take retribution on your property—or possibly go after…something else." Sheriff Bower turned toward Grace.

Grace squared her shoulders. "Me?" she squeaked.

The sheriff nodded. Richard pushed his chair back and sat up straighter. "Why do you believe Grace is in danger? What have you heard?"

"Nothing I can prove. Just rumors, but from very credible sources, and my gut. Some of the men I employ from time to time are voicing their concern about things they hear on the street. They're fairly certain Jorge has not left St. Augustine. And according to the law, he should still be in the area working on restitution."

Richard stood up and stationed himself behind her. Grace relished the nearness. He placed his hands on her shoulders. "I'll do whatever it takes to protect my wife, Sheriff."

"I know you will. Hopefully, this is all rumor aimed to make the two of you uneasy."

"Well, it's working," Grace mumbled.

Richard squeezed her shoulders. "I'll make sure no harm comes to you, Grace," he whispered into her ear. She patted the top of his hand. Just as she began to think her life would be normal, something like this had to happen.

"I'll see myself out. I'm sorry I didn't have better news. I'll also have my deputies keep an eye on the inn, extend their patrol areas for a week or so. We'll know by then if these are simply rumors or if they are a real threat." The sheriff put his hat on his head and walked toward the front room. He turned back toward them. "Congratulations on your marriage. I pray you'll be as happy as my wife and I have been. Good night."

It was hard knowing your marriage wasn't a real marriage and hearing encouragement like that. Grace closed her eyes and prayed that one day the sheriff's prayers would come true.

"I'm so sorry, Grace. I never meant for you to be in harm's way. I do believe Jorge will be after items he can sell, and he knows what I have at the inn."

Grace didn't mind him referring to the inn as his. She certainly hadn't gotten to the point of accepting that it also belonged to her, either. Richard tapped her shoulders then went back to his seat. "I'll see what I can do to have some additional eyes watching over you and the inn."

"Do you really believe I'm in danger?"

"Sheriff Bower wouldn't come and scare us for no reason. He's heard something to make him quite concerned."

Grace trailed her fork through her mashed potatoes. "You're right, he wouldn't." She took a breath and changed the subject. "How do you think Manny is doing in the hospital?"

"He's either got the staff in continuous laughter or they're about to strangle him. Manny can drive a person either way."

Grace chuckled. "True. I suspect he'll have the staff in a gay mood."

"I believe you're right. However—" Richard reached over and took her hand "—we need to discuss your safety. I will accompany you wherever you need to go."

"You won't get any work done. Or I won't. We can't live in fear. I can't live in fear," she amended.

Richard paused and stared at their hands. Then his gaze traveled up to her eyes. His eyes, she noticed, were hazel tonight. "I couldn't live with myself," he continued, "if something were to happen to you, and I didn't do everything I possibly could to protect you. You're too precious." He squeezed her hand and released it.

He sat back in his chair and placed his cloth napkin in his lap.

"I understand. However, I do not want to feel trapped and unable to travel about as I need to."

"I'll keep a respectful distance. But for most outings, I can simply be the adoring husband doting on his wife." Richard smiled.

They were getting closer with one another. Did he mean those words? Could she hope?

Grace nodded. "That will be fine." She leaned down to face her plate and hid any smile or twinkle of excitement she felt in hearing the words *doting on*. "Getting back to Manny, I'm thinking we'll have to add his laundry to ours. There were some items in there I doubt have ever been washed."

Richard shuddered. "Ew...not while I'm eating, Grace."

"My apologies. Growing up on a ranch, many far more descriptive things were a part of the dinner conversation."

"Hmm, I suppose my growing up was more high brow. Father was raised at the inn. So when we visited, he'd go over the table manners again and again before we visited with our grandparents. Naturally, I kept the same manners when taking care of my grandmother. I generally ate alone in the evenings, often going to a restaurant rather than cooking for myself."

Grace placed her fork beside her plate. "If we decide to take our marriage to the next level and we have children, would you want them raised in the same manner?"

Richard coughed, avoiding choking on his mouthful of food. "Children?" he squeaked.

"Yes," she whispered. Her head was bowed. "If we were to take our marriage to..."

Richard reached over and grasped her hand. "Grace,

I didn't mean to embarrass you. I was more shocked that you were even thinking about…children."

"I'm sorry. I know our marriage is a business arrangement but…" She glanced up at him. Tears welled up in her eyes.

"If…" he began cautiously. He would love to have children with Grace, but he had to be patient and wait upon her. "If we were to deepen our relationship, I would be honored to have children with you. As for how we shall raise them, let us first get to the point of…well, you know."

Grace smiled. Richard's heart thumped. *Lord, I am falling in love with this woman. Help me not be a disappointment to her.*

"Very well. Getting back to our other obligation, Manny. How do we encourage without wounding him, concerning the way he's kept his room?"

Richard sat back and picked up his fork. "I'll be frank with him concerning the matter. However, I believe your gentle way with words will win him over. We can speak of the health issues, and we can use his needing to go to the hospital as a way to convince him to live in a healthier environment. The man was terrified about going to the hospital."

"I noticed." Grace dabbed her lips with the linen napkin.

Richard wanted to kiss those delicate lips. He focused on his plate in front of him. While the food was delicious, it had lost its appeal. He forked a huge serving. He needed distraction. "I'm going to take care of Manny's medical expenses."

"You might not have to. While I was looking for laundry, I discovered he has a small fortune in there."

"A what?"

"Apparently, he doesn't like spending money. I found fifty dollars in one pocket, another thirty in another, and another fifty in another pocket. Then I ran across a small trunk with a padlock. I might be wrong, but it might be his bank."

"Interesting." Richard mumbled. "As you know, we only charge him ten dollars for the entire month. It's a special rate my grandmother arranged with him years ago."

Grace chuckled. "Well, a hundred and thirty dollars isn't going to keep the man well housed and fed for long, but he might have more money than you are aware of. Then again, it could be his entire worth. I simply don't know. I'm just cautioning you not to be too generous. He might have more funds than we are aware of."

Richard leaned back in his seat. "You're a wise woman, Mrs. Arman. You're quite an asset to me and the inn."

Grace smiled. "I'm glad I'm helping."

"More than you know. Thank you."

"You're welcome." Grace started to get up from the table. "I have some chores to get done before I call it a night. But I'll say good-night now."

"Leave your dishes in the sink, and I'll take care of cleanup tonight. You do what you need to do."

"Thank you, Richard."

"You're welcome." He watched as she walked into the kitchen with her plate and glass in hand. He was going to have a rough time sleeping tonight. The idea of children, caring for Manny and Grace's loving ways would keep his mind buzzing. Richard groaned. Perhaps marrying her wasn't the wisest plan. Then his mind drifted to Jorge. *Please, God, keep her safe.*

The next morning they all got to work on Manny's room. The extra help had the space cleared out by lunch. Grace made a meal as a thank-you to all of the men who helped. By the end of the day they had found over five hundred dollars in various pockets and nooks and crannies where Manny had stuffed the money. Then there were the two locked boxes. Those possibly contained even more cash. All in all, Grace had been right; Manny could take care of his own medical expenses. And while Richard would not break his grandmother's agreement with Manny, he would be careful not to assume Manny didn't have the means to provide for himself.

The following day Manny returned looking weak but with a little color. As Richard ushered him into his freshly cleaned room, Manny's face went crimson. But once he discovered where all his belongings were and heard how hard Grace had worked on making his room clean and fresh, all the blustering subsided. Manny thanked Grace repeatedly.

Richard sat down with him and discussed the matter of cleanliness, changing his bed sheets and washing his clothes. Manny was surprised that Grace would take on the responsibility, but agreeable. He even offered to pay Grace two dollars a week for doing his laundry.

That afternoon Richard escorted Grace to the lawyer's office. He was pleased that Grace had opened up about the entire case with him, and that she had given Mr. Greeley the authority to speak to him as well as herself concerning these matters.

"Thank you for coming with me," Grace said, and leaned in closer as he escorted her on the walkway past the old schoolhouse. He always grinned at the sight of the old anchor chained around the schoolhouse.

"Thank you for trusting me with such private information."

Grace came to a stop. Richard stopped, as well, waiting. She cocked her head to the right. "Richard, you are my husband."

He placed his hand over hers. "I know. I'm simply honored."

"What affects me will undoubtedly affect you, as well."

"I reckon you are correct. What do you want to do with the land, when the judge rules in your favor?"

"I don't know. I have no use for the land now. I suppose we could sell it and use the money for the inn."

"The inn is fine." Richard paused and contemplated what Grace had done by opening up her legal matters to him. "Grace, when we get home I'd like to go over the books with you. I believe you should be aware of all our assets."

"And I'll show you mine, as well. Although I don't have much, I was doing fairly well until my father..."

"Speaking of your father, has he or your mother contacted you since we married?"

"No," Grace sighed. "I suppose it's my fault. I haven't reached out to them, either. And I'm the one who left the house."

He guided her to the left and down a block before heading farther south toward the inn. "When the time is right, send them a letter and invite them to dinner at the Seaside Inn."

"You wouldn't mind?"

"No, absolutely not."

"Even after Father said those horrible things to you?"

"It does not matter. He was angry and uncertain of my intentions. Perhaps in time he'll see me as a good man."

"As my husband," Grace whispered, though it didn't escape his ears.

Changing the subject, Richard said, "I'm hoping to launch my sailboat in a couple of days."

"I can't wait. You do know I love to sail?"

"So you've said a time or two." He grinned. He was amazed at how many interests they both shared.

They walked up the front steps of the Seaside Inn. Sitting on the rocking chairs on the front deck were his parents. "Mother, Father, it's good to see you. This is such a surprise. May I present my wife, Grace." He escorted her to his mother, who leaped to her feet and gave Grace a warm hug.

His father, on the other hand, seemed quite perturbed.

## Chapter 13

Grace pried herself free from Richard's mother. She was about the same height as herself, and she could see where Richard inherited his hair and eyes. His chin definitely came from his father, as well as his overall build and stature. "I'm so happy to meet the woman who finally captured my son's heart," Mrs. Arman said.

"Pleasure to meet you, too, Mrs. Arman."

Richard embraced his mother. "It is good to see you, Mother." He turned toward his father and offered him his hand. The two men shook. "Father."

"When did you arrive?" Grace asked, feeling the awkward moment between father and son.

"The train arrived a half hour ago. We only arrived at the inn about five minutes ago," Mrs. Arman said.

"You should have wired us. I would have met you at the train," Richard offered.

"Your father and I wanted to surprise you. I hope it isn't an imposition."

"Of course not." Richard opened the front door.

"Come in, and I'll fix you something cool to drink," Grace offered. Richard's mother entered the house with noticeable ease and poise compared to the stiffness with which Mr. Arman walked in. He hadn't even said a word. She wondered if she was a disappointment to him.

Grace followed her in-laws, and Richard came in behind them all. "Please, sit in the parlor, and I'll bring you some fresh limeade." Grace hurried into the kitchen. She took some scones she'd made that morning and put them on a plate then placed it on a tray. Next, she slid the block of ice out of the icebox and chipped off some for their drink then grabbed the glass pitcher and placed the ice chips in the bottom. The fresh lime juice she had squeezed that morning she poured over the ice, stirring in a little sugar water. Four glasses finished off the tray. By the time she returned to the parlor, the others were settled in various chairs listening to Mrs. Arman talking about their trip.

Mr. Arman stood as she entered the room. "Sit, please," Grace encouraged. "We're family, no need for formalities. You've probably already told Richard this, but how long will you be staying?"

"For a few days," Mrs. Arman said as she reached for a glass and poured some limeade, then handed it to Mr. Arman and repeated the process again for herself. Grace wondered if she should be pouring Richard's glass. Richard leaned over and poured his own. Grace was too nervous to drink.

"It is a pleasure to meet you both."

"My son says you're a widow?" Mr. Arman asked. The first words carried an edge.

"Yes, sir. My husband was killed in the war."

"I'm sorry to hear that." His voice softened. "You have my condolences."

Grace nodded and sat down in a chair next to Richard.

"Richard, why don't I run to the butcher shop and pick up some steaks for dinner tonight?"

At that very moment, Manny walked into the room using a cane. Richard stood up. "How are you feeling, Manny?"

"Fine, fine. Sit down. I thought I heard familiar voices. It's good to see you, Melinda, John."

Grace watched as Melinda embraced Manny with as much enthusiasm as she had embraced her. "Forgive me for saying so, Manny, but you're looking pale. Are you all right?"

"Getting better every day. I…"

"Manny was sick enough that he had to go to the hospital," Richard interjected. "Doc says he's doing well now."

"Oh, my gracious!" Mrs. Arman embraced Manny again. "You take good care of yourself."

Manny chuckled. "I will. The missus—" Manny tilted his head toward Grace "—she takes real good care of me."

Grace smiled and noticed Richard's father relax for the first time. Grace leaned over to Richard and whispered, "Richard, shall I go fetch some steaks from the butcher?"

"Yes."

Grace stood up. "Excuse me. I'll be right back."

She hustled out the back door of the kitchen and over

to George Leonardy's butcher shop. "Good afternoon, Mr. Leonardy."

"Good afternoon, Mrs. Martin. How can I help you today?"

"I'm here to pick up some steaks for my husband and his family. By the way, I'm Mrs. Arman now. Richard Arman and I have married."

"Congratulations. You and Mr. Arman make a fine couple. So, how many steaks would you like?"

"Four Delmonico cuts, please."

George went back into the walk-in iced room. Grace paced. Her mind raced with what to cook, what Richard's father's concerns about her were and with how she and Richard could keep up the appearance of a normal marriage while not sleeping in the same room. They were progressing as a couple, they were even talking about the possibility of having children one day. But they were not a true married couple, and if anyone would be able to spot that it would be Richard's parents, especially staying in the same house together.

George came back with four beautifully cut Delmonico steaks on brown butcher paper. "How are these?"

"Beautiful. Thank you, George."

"How would you like to pay for these today?"

"I ran out without my purse. Let's charge it to the Seaside Inn account."

George's face contorted. "I'm sorry, I can't do that. Mr. Arman has exclusive orders that no one but himself can charge on the inn's account."

Grace knitted her eyebrows together then relaxed them remembering Jorge's thefts. "Oh, I understand. Can I charge them to myself and pay you in the morning?"

"Absolutely. And if Mr. Arman would come in and

approve you for the Seaside Inn, you would not have any problem charging on that account."

Grace smiled. "I'll mention that to him. Thank you, Mr. Leonardy." He handed over the brown wrapped paper tied with white cotton string. "I'll see you in the morning and take care of this."

"Have a good evening, Mrs. Arman."

"Thank you, Mr. Leonardy. Tell your wife I said hello." Grace left the shop and nearly ran back to the inn. As she turned the corner down the street, Jorge jumped out from behind some bushes and blocked her way. "Whatcha got there, Mrs. Arman?" he sneered.

She pushed past, startled but refusing to entertain him in conversation. She closed her eyes for a moment and picked up her pace. Her body wanted to react, to run. She forced herself to keep walking.

"Tell your husband I'm watching."

Richard couldn't believe the treatment Grace was receiving from his father. After she left, he confronted him. "How dare you treat my wife with such coldness? She's not done anything to offend you."

"Except she married you with no courtship. When is the child due?"

"John, really!" his mother admonished.

"She is not with child. We did not marry because I treated her improperly."

"Then why the rush? What happened to basic manners and propriety?" his father demanded.

"It was for the best. There are things I'm not at liberty to say. But I must ask you this, Father, when have I ever done anything inappropriate? I have met all of my obligations. I took care of Grandmother when no one else was willing to. I gave up my career to take care of her and…" Richard took a deep breath and let it out slowly. "You will respect my wife and give her the honor she deserves. She is a good and fine woman. A man could not ask for a better wife."

His father sat back.

"See, John, I told you Richard knows what he is doing." His mother placed a loving hand on his father's forearm.

"You are certain she is not after your money?"

"I am certain. She is about to inherit a hundred and twenty acres of land from her husband's estate. She does not need my money."

His father raised his eyebrows. A large crease crossed the top of the receding hairline. "Why so long? She said her husband died in the war, and that's been over for several years now."

"Again, this is her private information, and I am not at liberty to tell you unless she chooses to."

The back door of the kitchen slammed. "Richard," Grace cried out.

Richard bolted up and ran to the kitchen. Grace was shaking. "What's the matter?"

"Jorge met me on the road."

"Where? When? Are you all right?"

"Just a few moments ago. He was at the corner behind the house."

His parents joined them in the kitchen. Richard bolted out the door and ran down the street. "Jorge!" he shouted. He stopped and looked around. "I know you can hear me, Jorge," he yelled.

"You stay away from my wife. Come for me, be a man. Only weak-minded men go after another man's wife, you coward."

Richard waited for a response, looking in every direction. Hearing none, he ran back to the house. Grace was sitting in a chair where his father stood guard over her. His mother prattled around in the kitchen. "Thank you, Father." Richard came alongside and took her hand. His father wasn't a bad man, Richard knew. Although he could become very outspoken and stubborn once he made his mind up about something. Which appeared to be the case this time.

Grace looked up with her wonderful brown eyes. "Did you find him?"

"No, he's gone."

"I told your parents who Jorge is. I hope you don't mind."

Richard kissed the top of her head. "Not at all. Can I fix you some tea or something?"

"No, I'm fine."

"No, you're not. You go to your room to freshen up and I'll grill the steaks. Mother will cook up some sides."

"Richard, please, I'm fine. Let me prepare the meal for you and your parents. Although you do grill a better steak than I."

Richard wiggled his eyebrows. Grace giggled. "It's settled, then. You can cook the steaks. I'll take care of the kitchen. Oh, George Leonardy said you need to authorize me to purchase from his store."

"Right, I should have done that. I'm sorry. I'll take care of it tomorrow. How'd you pay for the steaks?"

"Mr. Leonardy let me charge them to myself. I told him I'd come by in the morning and settle the account."

"I'll give you the money. I'm sorry." Richard helped his wife from her seat and gave her an embrace. "I'm glad you're all right," he whispered in her ear.

She turned slightly and whispered in his. "So am I. I'm sorry I was so startled by Jorge."

"Nonsense. You did just fine. I'll send a message to Sheriff Bower." Grace nodded and stepped back.

His father cleared his throat. Grace blushed. "Sorry."

"Nonsense. You had quite a scare."

"Where's Manny?" Richard asked.

"I'm not sure," John answered. "He must have gone during all the commotion."

"Hmm," Richard responded. "Well, I'm sure he's fine. Let's get started on the meal."

Richard's mother put on an apron. "How can I help?"

"Do you folks like strawberry-rhubarb pie?" Grace asked.

Richard chuckled. "Yes, it's one of my father's favorites."

"Like father, like son?"

"When it comes to pie, yes," Richard admitted. He kissed her forehead. "I'll get the coals ready for the grill."

"I'll season the meat."

"And I'll get settled in our room." John stepped back. "Which room?"

Richard looked at Grace. "Five," he answered. How was he going to keep the secret that he and Grace were not a fully married couple yet? His father already wondered if Grace was out for his money.

His mother beamed. "And I'll help my new daughter in the kitchen."

Richard squeezed Grace's hand. "You're certain you are all right?"

"Yes. Thank you."

Richard nodded, a lump stuck in his throat.

He hurried off toward the backside of the barn and retrieved some wood to make the coals. He'd get a roaring fire going and let it burn down to some large coals for the grill. Normally he kept coals that could easily be ignited again with some small kindling. Today he needed to make large coals, and lots of them. It was early enough in the day to cut and burn down the wood.

Richard reached for his ax against the wall of the barn. It was not where it should be. He searched the area behind and around the barn but didn't find it. Finally, he searched inside. He stood and stared as dark thoughts formed. *Dear God, no.*

Grace decided to make her garlic mashed potatoes with some fresh green beans as well as some quick biscuits to fill out the meal. "You like to cook?" Mrs. Arman asked.

"Yes, ma'am. I enjoy it very much, and to have such a large kitchen to work in. It's wonderful."

Melinda Arman smiled. "Relax, honey. I'm not here to test you. I'm just so excited that Richard has found someone. We'd pretty much given up hope. Willa Jean hurt him deeply… Oh, dear, I'm sorry. I shouldn't have said anything."

"I know about Willa Jean just as Richard knows about my relationship with my husband, Micah."

Melinda raised her eyebrows.

"Former husband," Grace amended. "Forgive me. I've been a widow for a lot longer than I've been married to your son."

Melinda's smile returned. "I understand. Do you understand why John is so concerned about you?"

"I suspect it is because we married quickly."

Melinda nodded. Grace wasn't going to add to the conversation. Given Mr. Arman's disapproval, he'd certainly not understand the arrangement between her and Richard.

"Nooooo," a squeal from the backyard caught their attention.

Grace ran out the back door. Seeing the barn door open, she ran over and stopped. "Oh, no," she joined in Richard's lament. "What happened?"

Richard picked up the ax. "Jorge, I reckon."

"I'm so sorry. Can it be fixed?"

His parents joined them at the barn. "I'll get the sheriff." His father called out.

Grace couldn't believe the size of the hole Jorge—or whoever—had cut into the side of the boat, just below the waterline. There was no question this would take days if not weeks to fix. She walked up to Richard and wrapped her arms around him, laying her head on his back. "I'm so sorry, Richard. You've worked so hard."

He turned in her arms. "As have you. It can be repaired. I'm thankful for God's protection over you." He cupped her face in his hands. "Promise me you won't go out alone until the sheriff catches Jorge."

Grace saw the depth of concern and worry in Richard's eyes. "I promise." Any man that could take an ax to another man's property just because he'd been caught doing something illegal...well, Grace didn't want to be alone with Jorge ever again.

"Good." He pulled her to his chest and kissed the top of her head. She squeezed a bit tighter.

"Son, I'm sorry. I know how much work you've put into that boat." His mother's compassionate heart rang true. Richard stepped out of Grace's embrace but continued to support her with his arm draped over her shoulder.

"It's a disappointment, and I'm upset, but I'm more concerned with Grace's safety."

"Your father will get the sheriff. I'm certain they'll be able to catch this man." Richard released Grace and stepped away, picking up the ax. "Excuse me, ladies. I believe I need to chop some wood."

Mrs. Arman reached over to Grace and took her hand. "Come. He needs to work this out."

Grace hesitated but followed her mother-in-law back to the house and into the kitchen. Busy hands were probably best for her, as well. It was hard to believe everything that had happened in one day. She turned back to see Richard remove his coat and roll up his sleeves.

"What's all the ruckus?" Manny asked using the counter for support.

"Someone, probably Jorge, cut a hole in the side of Richard's boat."

"What?" Manny stomped out of the house and headed toward the barn.

Melinda Arman went to the counter and unwrapped the steaks. "Manny has a heart of gold. We never understood what Mother saw in him, but we've come to appreciate his intuition with regard to people."

"Richard and I have adopted him, like an eccentric uncle of a sort. Manny does have good intuition, but even he didn't see the true nature of Jorge and Eva."

"Things are certainly hopping. What can I do?" Melinda scanned the kitchen.

"I was going to make some biscuits to go with our dinner. Would you like to work on those?"

"Sure." Melinda cinched her apron and went to work. She knew where everything was in the kitchen, which of course made sense.

A half hour later Sheriff Bower came in. "Good afternoon, Mrs. Arman. Mr. Arman says you had a run-in with Jorge?"

"Yes, sir."

"Did he approach you?"

"Yes. He jumped out of the bushes, and he asked me what I had, which was the meat for tonight's supper. Then he told me to tell my husband that he was watching us."

Sheriff Bower removed his hat, wiped its inner band then leaned back on the kitchen counter. "I see. But he didn't try to reach for you or grab you in any manner?"

"No, sir. I didn't respond. I just kept walking."

"Good. Most would stop in fear, and others might try to engage in debate. And with Jorge's actions today, I'd say avoidance was the best policy. I'll have my men searching for him. We'll find him, and I'll lock him up."

Grace looked down at the floor, thinking, and then met his eyes. "Will the judge just let him go again?"

"Not this time. He's caused serious property damage and proved he wasn't remorseful for his actions. When I catch him, he'll be going to jail for a mighty long time."

"Good."

"Richard said he's advised you not to go out on your own. I want to reiterate the same advice. Be wise and be safe, Mrs. Arman."

"I will, Sheriff." The sheriff put his hat back on his head and turned to leave. "Have a good evening, Mrs. and Mrs. Arman."

"Good evening, Sheriff."

Richard's father came in as the sheriff departed. "Are you ladies all right?"

"We will be," Melinda supplied.

"When is dinner?" John asked.

"In two hours," Richard answered as he closed the screen door behind him.

"Then your mother and I will excuse ourselves for a while and freshen up after our travels."

Richard nodded.

"See you at five," Grace called out as the older couple left the room.

Richard came up beside her. "Grace, we need to talk," he whispered.

# Chapter 14

Richard grasped Grace's hand and led her to her room. "We have a problem."

"Sleeping arrangements?" She turned away from him.

"Yes. If it is all right with you, I'll sleep on the floor in here and my parents will be none the wiser."

"Wouldn't it be better to tell them the truth about our marriage?"

"No." He was on edge. He knew it. Chopping the wood had let off some steam, but he was still angry. He was angry before he found the damage to the boat. He was upset with his father and his accusations. Richard relaxed his tone. "It's my father. I don't want him to think poorly of you."

"I appreciate that," Grace said, and walked away from him. "We talked about the possibility of having children one day."

"Grace, don't," Richard pleaded.

She turned to face him then turned back to the window.

"Grace." Richard stepped up beside her. "As much as I would like to move forward with our marriage, I don't believe this is the time. I'm angry in a way that I haven't been for years. I would not want to soil any part of our relationship with this anger."

Grace turned and faced him. She searched his eyes, digging deeper into his soul. He'd never had this connection with another. "Can I help?"

"I don't know. How are you dealing with the anger concerning the Martins and what they've done to you?"

"With a lot of prayer. I, too, am angry, but I'm feeling more sad for them now. Today when we were at the lawyer's office… Can you believe that was only three hours ago?" Grace shook her head. "While we were there I was thinking how much I don't want that land. I mean, I need to go forward with the case in order to prove the point and prove that they were wrong and cheated me out of my inheritance, but I honestly don't want that land. It's spoiled. I no longer see it as a provision from my husband but rather an instrument that proved that his parents didn't care for me. Does that make sense?"

"Yes. Yes, it does. Whatever you decide to do with the land once the judge settles the matter, I'm behind you. As for me, I haven't been this angry since Willa Jean's betrayal. Grace, I've grown to care for you deeply, very deeply. But Willa Jean's words still ring in my ears. She said I would never understand a woman, and I'm not worthy of being a husband. I've sheltered myself from ever getting close to another woman. Then you came along… and, well…" Richard paused. "I really like you, Grace.

Forgive me. This is not what we agreed upon when we decided to marry."

She stepped toward him. He wrapped her in his arms. "Nor did I, Richard. But my feelings for you have grown, as well."

"Good, then I shall spend the evening on the floor, if you don't mind."

"I do mind. I think it is horribly unfair for you to sleep on the floor. We are married."

Richard shook his head. "No, it would not be prudent. I have spent many a night on a bedroll. I will be fine."

Grace nodded. They both weren't ready for that commitment to one another. On the other hand, Richard wouldn't mind...then again, was he really worthy of Grace's love? Of any woman's love? Willa Jean had left her mark on his soul. Even after all these years, her negative taunts were still haunting him. He inwardly shook off the thoughts. He couldn't live in the past. He had a future, and it was with Grace, his wife, the woman who committed herself to him for better and worse. He simply prayed she would not receive the worse.

"What's the matter?" she asked.

"I'm sorry. Willa Jean," was all he could answer.

"Richard, I don't know about everything Willa Jean said or did to you but please understand you are a fine man, a wonderful husband. A woman couldn't ask for better."

His heart soared. "But you have not seen me at my worst."

"Nor have you seen me at mine, and hopefully, that will never happen. On the other hand, if we continue to get closer, then the probability is high that we will disappoint one another from time to time."

Richard chuckled. "You're a wise woman, Grace Arman."

She winked and pinched his cheek. "And don't you ever forget it. Now, I'd better get back to the kitchen before our supper is ruined."

"And I should get to those coals. They should be just about ready."

They left the room and headed to the kitchen where they found Manny checking the various pots and bowls. "Looks like a grand feast."

"Would you like to join us for dinner tonight, Manny?" Grace asked.

"Got enough?"

"Of course. When has my wife left us at the table not filled to overflowing?"

"I can't say I remember a time." Manny tapped his belly. "You're sure it isn't a problem."

"It's not a problem, Manny. We'll be eating at five," Grace offered.

"Great. By the way, I'll accompany Grace wherever she needs to go. I'll be carrying protection just in case."

"Accompanying will be sufficient. I don't want guns involved. Someone might get hurt," Richard warned.

"That's the idea. I'm a pretty fair shot."

"I imagine you are, but you still don't have your strength back and, judging by the rust I saw on your pistol, I'd say it's been a while since you shot it, let alone cleaned it."

"You know, when ya didn't know everything I owned, you wouldn't have said such a thing," Manny responded.

Grace placed a loving touch on Manny's forearm. "Manny, I appreciate your willingness to protect me.

However, I think Richard is right. We don't want to make Jorge more angry than he already is."

Manny sighed. "I suppose you're right. Sheriff said something 'bout the same."

"Then let us be wise. Now, why don't you clean up and then you can help me set the table," Grace suggested.

Richard squeezed Grace's hand. He couldn't believe her capacity to love others. He wanted to believe that she loved him, although she hadn't proclaimed her love in so many words. Nor had he proclaimed his love to her. But he knew he loved her, and with each passing day, he discovered another way to love her. *Please, Father God, keep her safe. Protect her from Jorge. Protect her from me.*

Grace still couldn't believe the turnaround in Richard's father from the moment he arrived until the moment when they said goodbye three days later. He seemed to completely accept her and was happy with Richard's choice of a spouse.

Jorge had been caught and was now awaiting trial in jail. It was safe for her to walk to the markets and shop for the Seaside Inn. Tonight was their first dinner alone since his parents had arrived, and she was going all out with a special dinner. She entered George Leonardy's butcher shop. Ignacia, his wife, was standing behind the counter. "Good morning, Mrs. Arman. My George, he told me that you and Mr. Arman are married now. Congratulations."

"Thank you, Mrs. Leonardy. I've come to get some lamb chops for dinner tonight. And I'll need ten pounds of bacon and ten pounds of mild breakfast sausage, as well, for the inn."

"I'll be happy to get that for you. Will you be paying for this yourself or charging to your account?"

"Charge it to the Seaside. Richard should have come in and approved me."

"I'm sorry, Mrs. Arman, your husband has not come in yet. I'm certain it is an oversight. I can charge these to you, and your husband can come in and pay for it later."

"Oh, dear. I thought he would have taken care of it by now." Grace reached into her purse. "How much will this come to?"

"Five or six dollars."

Grace rummaged through her purse and found the cash she needed. "I can purchase the items."

"I'm so sorry," Ignacia said as she went to work cutting the appropriate amount of bacon and sausage. Then she pulled out a small rack of lamb chops. "Would you like them cleaned or would you like to do that?"

"I'll clean them. With the bits and pieces I cut off I'll make a stew."

"Very well." Ignacia weighed the chops and then wrapped them in brown paper and tied it together with the white cotton string, as with every meat package from Leonardy's butcher shop.

Grace paid for the meat and took her packages, placing them inside her canvas bag that she flung over her shoulder. "Good day, Mrs. Leonardy."

"Good day, Mrs. Arman, and I am certain your husband will be in soon to clarify your account."

Grace nodded. Why would Richard forget to come by? She supposed it could be because of his parents' visit. She would forgive him this time and remind him again of the need to have him put her on the charge account. Or, if he was not comfortable with her charging meat, then he'd have to make the daily trips to the butcher shop. Time was limited for Richard. He was working night and day on this boat, repairing the damage that Jorge had done.

Grace stopped by the vegetable market and found some fresh vegetables. There was fresh mint and dill in the herb garden at the inn. She'd harvest what she would need for the lamb. Then she spotted a large stalk of Brussels sprouts and purchased it, as well.

She threaded her way through the narrow streets and headed back to the Seaside Inn. "Grace, can I help you?" Manny met her at the door, reached out and relieved her of some of her burdens. "What did you purchase today?"

"Lamb chops. I'm going to save the pieces I cut off for some lamb stew."

"Yum. I wish I was going to be here for dinner." Manny cocked his head to the right. "Ah, you planned a romantic dinner for you and your husband since you knew I was going out with my buddies tonight."

Grace winked. "Possibly. Where is he?"

"Front desk. Well, I'm off. Save me some of that stew."

"Tomorrow night's dinner."

Manny rubbed his stomach. "Lookin' forward to it." And with that, Manny slipped out the door and was gone.

Grace put her bundles on the counter and went to the front desk. "Hi, I'm back if you'd like to work in the barn."

Richard smiled. "Thank you." He reviewed which rooms were available and who was planning to eat breakfast in the morning.

"Speaking of breakfast, I was at George Leonardy's butcher shop, and I wasn't able to charge to the Seaside Inn account yet."

"I'm sorry. I forgot all about it with my parents here

and that business with Jorge. I'll take care of it in the morning."

"Wonderful. Here's the receipt for what I spent today. I had enough cash on me to take care of it."

Richard scanned the receipt. His head came up. "Lamb chops?"

"Yes. I know how much you love them."

"Thank you." He reached into the cash drawer and pulled out what she'd spent and gave it to her. "Here, you don't have to be spending your cash for the Seaside."

*Well then, don't forget to authorize me to charge.* She held back her thoughts and took the proffered money. "Go work on your boat. I'll take care of the inn."

He hustled off to his room to change his clothes. Grace checked the bell over the door then headed into the kitchen. She had a lot of preparation to do for tonight's dinner. She would pan fry the chops. She trimmed off the extra layer of meat and set it aside for the stew, then took a piece of string and wrapped it around the bone of the chop and pulled the meat off the tip of the bone. Those pieces were also set aside for the next day's stew. Then she prepared the marinade of mint, dill, olive oil, salt, pepper, minced garlic, vinegar, water, crushed red pepper and a teaspoon of honey. She spooned the marinade on both sides of each chop and placed them on a shallow pan, covered it and placed them in the icebox. Then she prepared the bacon, cutting it into thin strips for the morning breakfast. The bacon could be done in the morning, but anything she could get done ahead of time helped the morning meal go smoother.

The bell over the front door jangled. Grace wiped her hands on a towel and removed her apron. "Good afternoon, how may I help you?" she said as she walked in without taking note of who was standing there. "Mother?"

Richard dusted himself off after working all afternoon in the barn. The new boards were in place. The gluing and sanding were taking shape, and he was ready to begin applying the layers of paint. With any luck he'd have the boat ready next week. He rested easier knowing Jorge was behind bars and would be staying there for a mighty long time. Since his first arrest for the thefts, other sheriffs had contacted Sheriff Bower and discovered that the man they were looking for was the same as Jorge. After he finished his sentence in Florida, he would be transported back to Alabama and await trial there.

Richard closed the barn door and locked it with the large padlock he'd purchased. He wasn't taking any chances. He walked into the kitchen. Grace was not there. He worked his way to the front desk then the parlor. "Mrs. Flowers, it's a pleasure to see you," he greeted his mother-in-law.

"Thank you, Mr. Arman. I hope you don't mind, but I wanted to visit with my daughter."

"It is not an imposition. You're welcome to visit anytime."

She looked down at her lap. "What about Mr. Flowers?" she asked.

"He's welcome, as well."

Helen Flowers lifted her gaze to his. He knew visits with Mr. Flowers would be awkward at first, but it couldn't be any worse than it had been with his father last week. Helen smiled. "Thank you, Mr. Arman. That is most kind of you."

Richard nodded.

"Mother, I'm making lamb chops. Would you care to stay for dinner?"

Helen glanced at the clock on the mantel. "Oh, gracious, no. I must get home and prepare your father's dinner."

"Would you and Mr. Flowers care to join us for Sunday dinner after church?" Richard walked over and stood beside Grace.

Helen smiled again. "Thank you. That would be wonderful. I'll check with Henry and send you a message."

"Wonderful. Now, if you ladies will excuse me, I need to clean up and get rid of these dusty work clothes." Richard gave a slight bow and walked back to his room where he washed and changed. He stood in front of the mirror and arranged his tie. The desire to dress his best for Grace grew day to day. He adjusted his collar and wrapped the green tie around his neck with a barrel knot in front. It wasn't the typical way to wear a tie, but he'd seen it in a men's fashion gazette and decided he liked the look. Not to mention, Grace seemed to like it, as well. Then, of course, he didn't have to worry about food soiling a tie when it was fashioned in this way. He finished his outfit with a green vest and brown jacket that had a velour upper lapel. His dark green trousers with black pinstripes completed the outfit.

His grandmother always said he had an eye for fashion. And while he enjoyed looking neat for the customers, he especially wanted to look nice for Grace this evening. It was their first evening alone since his parents had left. They had so many things to discuss. Sleeping on her floor, knowing she was only inches away, had been difficult at first. Then he found a comfort in hearing her say good-night to him just before she fell off to sleep. How was it possible to fall more in love with a person just hearing them breathe while they slept? He didn't understand it, but he knew it to be true. He didn't know if he was ready to admit his love for Grace to her yet, but he felt it coming. Soon he'd have to confess his feelings and attraction before he did something foolish and blurted it out at an inappropriate time or place.

Richard tugged his sleeves and inspected himself one more time in the mirror. Satisfied, he exited his room and found his wife in the kitchen.

She turned and faced him. Her smile, the twinkle in her eyes, said all the extra primping had been worth it. "My, aren't you handsome tonight."

*Handsome?* His heart raced. "Thank you. And if I may be so bold, I dressed for you."

Pink infused Grace's cheeks. "Then in that case, would you mind setting the table and watching the chops while I make myself more presentable."

"You're beautiful just the way you are, but I don't mind."

Grace slipped off the apron and handed it to him. He placed hers on the pole and retrieved his own, took a glance at the chops in the pan and went into the dining room. He opened his grandmother's private stock of china and selected a couple of plates from the finest set. He placed her best silver beside the plate then proceeded to take two of the finest crystal glasses that were seldom used and placed them on the table. He went back into the kitchen to check on the lamb chops and flipped them over. They were perfect. He removed the pan from the hot surface so they wouldn't overcook.

Grace came in with a dark green skirt, almost the same color as his trousers. The bottom of the skirt had a black hem six inches deep. The skirt was full but didn't have a full bustle, which he appreciated. He thought bustles were extremely foolish and impractical. She had a white blouse with a waistcoat of the same green-and-black design over the blouse. She also wore a string of white pearls. He took her hands in his. "Simply stunning, Grace. You take my breath away."

The pink glow of her cheeks deepened. "Thank you."

He wanted to wrap her in his arms and kiss her. Instead he turned his attention back to their dinner. "The lamb chops are ready."

"I'll get the sides if you can put the chops on our plates."

"At your service, madam."

Grace giggled. He fled through the dining room doors before he said something foolish, like admitting his love for her. He set two chops on her plate and three on his. He had to respect a woman who knew how to eat and enjoy food. He placed the pan on the cart and waited for Grace, holding her chair out for her.

Grace took in a deep breath and let it out slowly. Did she dare hope that tonight would bring them closer? *Father, help us,* she silently prayed as she pushed through the kitchen doors and stepped into the dining room. He'd set the table with his grandmother's best china and crystal. Her heart soared.

The rest of the evening was filled with wonderful tenderness between them. Their relationship was progressing, and Grace couldn't have been happier.

"Shall we take a walk before we retire for the evening?" Richard stood up and offered her his hand. "I don't mind showing off the most beautiful woman in town as my bride." He winked.

"I'd love to, but what about the dishes?"

"I'll take care of them later," he offered. "For now I want to enjoy this evening with you."

"And I with you." She stood and cradled her arm in his as he escorted her out of the dining room, down the front stairs and out onto the street. The sun was setting behind them. The sky was alive with purple and pink clouds. Grace nuzzled closer. "This is nice."

"Very." He placed his hand upon hers.

"Richard?" "Grace?" They both began at once.

"You go first," Richard offered.

Grace took in a shallow breath and exhaled. "Richard, forgive me, but I've fallen in love with you."

Richard stopped and turned her in his arms. "And I you. There is nothing to forgive. However, this is not the place to speak of such personal matters."

Grace scanned the area. People were busy going to and fro, from shop to shop and business to business. "Where can we have a personal conversation?" she asked.

"At home."

"Where? The front parlor is for the guests as well as family. I don't understand how your grandparents raised a family and maintained an inn. When and where was their private time?"

Richard turned and headed back toward the inn. "Father told me that the front parlor was once half its present size for the guests, that there was once a wall that divided the rooms. And Grandmother didn't always provide breakfast. When the business was small, the family part of the house was kept strictly for family. After my father and his siblings left, my grandparents did some reconstructing of the rooms."

"Would you be willing to give up some of those rooms for us? I mean if we were to have a family?"

He held her tighter. "I would be happy to close off some of the rooms. How large of a family would you like?"

Grace let out a nervous chuckle. "I don't know. I always wanted brothers and sisters."

"Grace, before we take the next step in our marriage, there are some things you need to know about me. Like what happened with Willa Jean."

"If you must tell me, that is fine. But it is in the past. Do you wish to know about my relationship with Micah?"

"Only what you feel the need to share with me. I don't have a problem with your having been married before. From everything you've shared, you loved Micah and perhaps still do. I know I am not him but..."

She placed her finger to his lips. "You are more. I suspect that if Micah had lived, he would have matured into a fine man. But we were so young when we married. We had so much growing up to do."

"I still do," Richard teased.

Grace chuckled. "I suppose I do, as well."

Richard took in a deep breath and let it out slowly. Grace concentrated on him, soaking in every movement to better understand this man she was falling in love with.

"I've given you the basic details of Willa Jean's shenanigans. But she manipulated me in such a way that I believed her lies about me, that I was unworthy, did not know how to love a woman properly, that there was something wrong with how I thought and acted. I've come to realize from living with you and your gentle words of encouragement to me that there wasn't anything wrong with me but rather with her and with our relationship. My only fear is that I will not treat you as a man should."

Grace stopped near the steps to the Seaside Inn and turned him to face her. "Richard, you must understand something before we cross that threshold. You are the man I need. God blessed us with each other before we were even ready to accept it. You help me be a better person. You trust my judgment. You've opened your home, the details of your business and your heart to me. I love you, and I will never be sorry that I married you, or even for the way our marriage came together."

Richard swooped her up and twirled her around then set her back down. "And I love you, Mrs. Arman. May I kiss you?"

"Please," Grace giggled.

He bent down and placed his lips tenderly upon hers. She pulled him closer. Their kiss deepened. He picked her up in his arms and carried her up the stairs and through the front door.

Grace's heart raced. He brought her to their bedroom and closed the door. Tonight their marriage would be complete. It was time, and she was ready to accept that she was more than Micah Martin's widow. She was complete in herself and now Richard's wife—but more than that, his partner, friend and lover.

# Chapter 15

Richard woke early the next morning and cleaned up the dining room and kitchen before the customers came down for breakfast. He decided he would let his bride sleep, and he'd take care of this morning's meal. And if he was lucky enough to have her sleep in, he'd bring her breakfast in bed. He couldn't stop praising the Lord for the gift of Grace as his wife.

"Good morning," Manny said as he came into the kitchen. "Grace took out the fine china for your dinner last night, huh?"

Richard smiled. "She did an excellent job on the lamb chops."

"Don't remind me. She did say she was going to make lamb stew for tonight's dinner." Manny leaned against the sink. "Is she feeling all right?"

"She's fine. I just thought I'd let her sleep in." At that, Grace stumbled in with her housecoat on.

"Go back to bed, sweetheart. I'm taking care of breakfast this morning."

"Are you sure?" Grace rubbed her eyes and yawned. Richard smiled. "Absolutely."

"Thank you." Grace turned and headed back to their room.

A knock at the back door turned Richard's attention away from his wife. Manny went over and opened it.

"Is Grace here?" A woman with red hair and swollen green eyes stepped into the kitchen.

"She's not presentable for guests right now. How can I help you?" Richard asked.

"It's a personal matter, Mr. Arman. Grace is my best friend, and I need her advice."

"Why don't you have a cup of coffee and some breakfast? Then I'll get Grace."

"Smells wonderful. Are you making pancakes?" she asked.

"Yup, and we have some of Grace's blueberry syrup if you'd like."

"Yum." The young woman brightened. "If you don't mind."

"Be happy to serve you. Manny, would you escort... What is your name?"

"Sorry, Hope Lang." Richard rolled her name around in his brain trying to remember if Grace had ever spoken about her. Having no remembrance, he wondered if Hope was Grace's best friend, as well.

"Would you escort Miss Lang to the dining room?"

"Certainly. Do we have any other female guests?" Manny inquired.

"Mrs. Wend and her children will be with us for a few days. They should be down any minute."

Manny nodded. "Miss Lang." He extended his hand in the direction of the dining room doors.

All morning Richard had been thinking about how the house was originally sectioned off from the inn and wondering just how he was going to rearrange the rooms. One thing was certain, he and Grace deserved their privacy, as would their children whenever that day should come.

Breakfast went quickly. Richard let Grace know about her friend Hope after the first round of pancakes made their way to the table. Grace was dressed and out of the room fifteen minutes later. The two women secluded themselves in the back corner of the parlor. Every time Richard came out with more food, he noticed that Hope was crying, and Grace was being a compassionate friend. He wondered if there was anything he could do but accepted that as a man there probably wasn't.

Hope left before the final breakfast plate was served. Grace came into the kitchen and stole a strip of bacon from the platter. "Good morning, husband." She winked.

"Good morning, wife. Is there anyone left to feed?"

"Yes."

Richard sighed.

"Me," Grace teased.

Richard snatched her up and twirled her in the kitchen.

"You really should stop doing that." She beamed.

"Not as long as I have a strong back. I've been thinking. What if we close the inn for a week and take a sail. Just you and me, a honeymoon, if you wish."

"I'd love to. Can we afford to close the inn for a week?"

"Yes. In fact, it's time we talked about finances. I am not what some people would consider wealthy but I am not lacking in funds. I save most of my income, and I have other sources of income from back home."

"Oh."

"No secrets, Grace. I don't want you to ever feel like I'm not being honest with you. I don't know why Micah hid the purchase of the land from you. Perhaps he wanted to surprise you, not thinking anything would happen to him."

Grace stepped out of his embrace. "You're probably right. But I'll be honest, it still bothers me."

"I understand. If you don't mind, I'd like to come with you to court this morning."

She turned and faced him. "Thank you. I don't know how I will react when I see Micah's parents. I want to believe I'll behave in a Christian manner but…"

Richard came up beside her. "You can lean on me or squeeze my hand rather than say something you shouldn't."

Grace let out a nervous chuckle. "I can squeeze pretty hard. I've been a laundress for a year now. Wringing out sheets and towels strengthens ones hands."

"I can take it." At least he hoped he could. He slipped his arms around her and kissed her. "Good morning, sweetheart."

She snuggled into him. "Good morning, love."

The rest of the morning went quickly. Richard and Grace cleaned up the dishes. She took care of the beds and rooms. Richard moved his belongings into their room. She started the laundry then changed into appropriate clothing for meeting with the judge. She dressed in one of her fancier dresses, white and blue with a ruffled skirt.

Richard winked as he carried the last of his outfits into the room and hung them in the closet. "I'm a lucky man to have such a beautiful wife."

"Thank you. And if you don't mind my saying so, you're a stunning man." It was his turn to blush.

They arrived at the courthouse with fifteen minutes to spare. They sat on the bench outside and waited.

"How are you doing?" he asked.

"Fine. I just want this to be over."

William Sears walked up dressed in a dark three-piece business suit and holding a gentleman's cane. "Good morning, Mrs. Arman, Mr. Arman."

"Good morning, Mr. Sears."

He cleared his throat. "I must apologize for my behavior when we first met. My attorney has informed me of your husband's family's betrayal and that you did not know about his financial dealings. You have my sympathies."

"Thank you." Grace paused and reached for Richard's hand. "Mr. Sears, do you know why Micah needed to borrow money from you?"

Mr. Sears relaxed his stance. "He told me it was to settle the back taxes on the property he'd inherited."

"Thank you." Grace rolled her shoulders then glanced at Richard and mouthed the word "Inherited?"

Mr. Greeley walked up with his black valise. He greeted Grace first then the men. "Shall we?"

Grace nodded. Richard held out his elbow, and she clung to him. He placed his hand upon hers and felt her relax a smidgen more. He was thankful that the Martins had agreed to a private hearing in front of the judge rather than a trial. He didn't want Grace to be the subject of local gossip or to endure a public spectacle, even if she was in the right. Richard held out the chair for Grace to sit in. He sat beside her, and Mr. Greeley took the chair on her other side.

The Martins came in with their attorney. Grace stiffened. Richard placed his arm around his wife's chair. Again, he felt her relax. "Thank you," she whispered.

The judge walked in and sat behind his desk.

Grace closed her eyes and prayed one last prayer that this entire mess with Micah's parents would be over. The judge glanced down at the paperwork. "I've reviewed the material presented by all three attorneys, and I'm afraid this is an open-and-shut case. Mr. and Mrs. Martin, you are ordered to give the property to your son's widow. Your son's will is explicit in the matter, and I have no patience for people who would deny the last requests of their loved ones."

The judge turned toward Mr. Sears. "Your request for the six acres is granted. The promissory note that Mr. Micah Martin gave you has been verified as his signature so I'm ordering six acres of the hundred and twenty be sold immediately, and the money from the sale be given to you to satisfy Mr. Martin's debt."

Grace cleared her throat. "Your honor, can the Martins purchase the six acres and give the money to Mr. Sears?"

"There is nothing in my order that will prevent them from buying the land. In fact, if you wish to sell the land to them, you are free to do that."

"Thank you, your honor." For the first time in months, Grace felt relief. The judge had seen the injustice she'd been experiencing since learning about this land. The Martins had betrayed her. Most of all, they had dishonored Micah and his requests.

"I'm not paying for that land," Chalmer Martin sneered. "The land belongs to me. Always has, always will."

"Chalmer, stop. Your brother gave Micah that land, and Micah gave it to his wife. You have to accept that," Gemma pleaded with her husband.

Chalmer grumbled.

Richard tightened his hold on Grace. She looked over into his hazel eyes. Goodness, she loved this man. He was so different from Micah, then again he was also as kind as Micah had been to her.

The judge smacked his gavel on his desk. Grace jumped. "Mr. Martin, are you telling me you are going to refuse my orders? I'll be happy to put you in jail until you agree. Or better yet, we can have a public hearing on the matter and let the entire community know how you disrespected your son and cheated his wife."

"No, sir," Chalmer mumbled.

"Do you want the six acres Mrs. Arman is offering?"

"Yes, your honor," Gemma spoke up.

"Pay Mr. Sears three hundred dollars and the land will be yours."

"Three..." Gemma slapped Chalmer's knee and his mouth clamped shut. "Yes, sir."

"Mrs. Arman, the land is yours to do with as you wish."

"Thank you, sir."

"Dismissed." The judge got up from his desk and walked out the back door of his chamber. Gemma ushered her husband out. Their lawyer followed behind.

Mr. Sears placed his gloves on his hands. "I wish you no ill will, Mrs. Arman. I'm sorry for all the discomfort I've caused."

"You're forgiven, Mr. Sears. You had no idea how complicated this situation was and that others were involved."

He took her hand and smiled. "Congratulations on your marriage."

"Thank you."

Mr. Sears and his attorney left, leaving Richard, Grace and Ben Greeley alone in the judge's chambers. Richard turned to the attorney. "Mr. Greeley, I need to come by your office and change my will."

"You wish to add your wife as your beneficiary?"

"Yes, sir. I should have done it weeks ago."

"I'll have the paperwork drawn up, and you can come in next week."

"Thank you."

"You're welcome." Mr. Greeley turned toward Grace. "Mrs. Arman, I'll have the title to the property put in your name later this week."

"Thank you."

Mr. Greeley left. Richard offered his elbow. "How are you feeling now?"

"All right, I suppose. There was little to say or do. I should have taken your suggestion and had Mr. Greeley represent me alone. I didn't need to be here. I can't believe how angry Mr. Martin is toward me."

"Personally, I think he's more upset with his brother giving the land to Micah."

Richard led them out of the courthouse. Mrs. Martin stood at the bottom of the steps. "Grace, may I have a word with you?"

Richard gave her a silent look that questioned whether it was all right, to which she nodded. "Yes." Grace stepped away from her husband and joined her former mother-in-law.

"Grace, I'm sorry for the things I said to you a while back. I know you and Micah loved one another."

"Thank you for acknowledging that." Grace's voice caught in her throat.

"Also, we never meant to keep the land from you. I mean, well I can see how it looks like we kept it from you, but Chalmer has been using that acreage since we purchased our land. It never occurred to him that his brother would give it to his son. That isn't an excuse. But the first year after Micah died, we didn't even think about the land. It had always been a part of ours. Which, of course, it wasn't...but...well, please try to understand we weren't trying to keep the land from you, exactly.

"Oh, I'm making a mess of all of this. I'm sorry. I'm sorry for the hurt we caused you when you were grieving the loss of Micah. I have no excuse. I was grieving for my son, and I gave little thought to anyone for that first year. After that you moved back in with your parents and never came by. I just assumed you didn't want to see us. In either event, I am sorry.

"Returning the tablecloth spoke of your true heart. We were wrong, and I pray that someday you will forgive us."

"You're forgiven. I'm sorry for not coming to visit you, as well. Micah's death was hard to live with." Grace hugged her former mother-in-law.

"God bless you, Grace, and I'm glad you've found someone and have married again."

"Goodbye, Mrs. Martin. God bless you, too."

Grace held back the tears. Five years of grief and anger welled to the surface. It was over. Her life with the Martins was forever severed. She turned toward Richard.

Grace snuggled closer. The past was over, her future wide open with possibilities. But more than that, it was alive with love and peace. "Richard, is it all right if I give the Martins the land?"

"Sweetheart, I told you before, you can do whatever you'd like with the land. Are you certain? Is this what you really want to do?"

"Yes. I don't need it. Micah's family does."

He kissed the top of her head. "Yes, I believe you're right."

Grace sighed. His smile covered the pain as a healing balm.

"Come, my love. We have a honeymoon to plan." He reached out his hand, and she slipped hers in his.

"Yes, we do. A sail in the moonlight, alone on the boat, just you and me. Can we make that an annual event? Once a year we close the inn and…"

Richard guffawed. "Life with you will be an adventure, Mrs. Arman."

"And with you, Mr. Arman. You didn't answer my question." She wiggled her eyebrows.

"Yes, my love, we can close the inn at least once a year and take a vacation on the sea, on the land, anywhere you would like to go. I'm yours."

"And I'm yours. I love you, Richard."

Rather than answer her, he spun her in his arms and kissed her soundly on the lips. Grace's heart raced… calmed all at the same time. She never would have believed she could love again and to love so thoroughly.

"Come, my love." He tightened his grip and led with her down the street.

"Let's close the inn and celebrate." Grace giggled. "How soon can we launch that boat?"

\* \* \* \* \*

# REQUEST YOUR FREE BOOKS!

## 2 FREE INSPIRATIONAL NOVELS
## PLUS 2
## FREE
## MYSTERY GIFTS

*Love Inspired*

LIDIR13R

# REQUEST YOUR FREE BOOKS!

## 2 FREE INSPIRATIONAL NOVELS
## PLUS 2
## FREE
## MYSTERY GIFTS

*Love Inspired.*
### HISTORICAL
INSPIRATIONAL HISTORICAL ROMANCE